D0914549

THE
MONUMENT
MAKER

THE MONUMENT MAKER

Ronald Joseph

DOUBLEDAY & COMPANY, INC., GARDEN CITY, NEW YORK 1972

Athens Regional Library
Athens, Georgia

All of the characters in this book are fictitious,
and any resemblance to actual persons, living or dead, is purely
coincidental.

Library of Congress Catalog Card Number 78–175384
Copyright © 1972 by Ronald Joseph
All Rights Reserved
Printed in the United States of America
First Edition

WITH LOVE TO LENA BENNETT

.

172233

THE
MONUMENT
MAKER

CHAPTER ONE

For the past half hour, Roseanne Woodley had been driving proudly up and down Landry's Main Street, noisily showing off her brand-new Cadillac. She was taking no chances that the big two-tone green car would be overlooked. Every block or so she fired off a staccato ratatat on the horn and waved so vigorously at everyone she passed that her left arm ached.

After her dozenth full circuit, people on the sidewalks began to feel silly waving back at her for the third or fourth time. Closing their ears to the repeated honking and the roaring engine, they headed resolutely back to attend to their business, no longer looking up as she streaked by.

Smiling contentedly, Roseanne decided on one final pass before heading home, on the off chance that someone along the street had missed the display. She was halfway through the town's little business district when, out of the corner of her eye, she spotted the gaunt, stringy figure of her brother, Witt Tyler, marching past the storefronts in the direction of the bank.

She grabbed the steering wheel with both hands and gave it a violent twist, ignoring the cattle truck she forced onto the sidewalk as her Cadillac barreled through a two-wheeled

1

U-turn in the intersection. With a jarring squeal, the car lurched to a stop at the curbside ahead of Witt.

The horn blared so clamorously that passers-by looked up despite themselves, alarmed, afraid she was in trouble. All except Witt: he knew Roseanne too well. She was only trying to get his attention.

He strolled on past, poker-faced, his eye fixed straight ahead; and though it was his one and only eye he would have traded it eagerly for another in the back of his head so he could relish her expression. Roseanne wasn't used to being ignored.

The horn silenced abruptly, Roseanne's incredulous response to the snub. Witt giggled to himself imagining her furious eyes and the thin red thread of her angry lips. He didn't like Roseanne, couldn't remember a time in his life when he had; but somewhere along the line the two of them had settled into a sort of game. Somewhere between the time he had been cut out of his father's will and years later, when he bounced back thumbing his nose at the entire family by striking oil, he and Roseanne had squared off in a personal duel. As far as Witt was concerned, he did it for the fun of it. He suspected, however, that Roseanne took the game more seriously.

He didn't mind. It amused him, their snarling tug-of-war that went on year after year without either of them dragging the other across the line. What were the stakes after all? How serious could it get?

He walked on, showing her his back, enraging her. She leaned again into the horn, giving her end of the rope a sharp yank. Witt grinned and yanked back by stepping off the curb, increasing the distance between them.

A salvo of furious toots barraged him. He marched on, almost prancing, delighted to have riled her.

2

When he reached the bank on the next corner, he pushed through the glass doors and stepped inside.

If it had been 1848, instead of one hundred years later, his appearance would have terrified the tellers, men diving for cover scrambling for the Colts. He looked like an over-the-hill, but still dangerous, desperado, six and a half feet of skin and bones from his hand-tooled Mexican leather boots to his sweat-ringed Stetson's battered crown.

He was sixty-eight, but so thin and wasted, so lined, creased, and baked brown by the South Texas sun that people would have missed guessing his age by a decade or two. The knobby wrists of his long arms hung a good six inches past the frayed cuffs of his snap-button shirt. His hands were so big he could grasp a watermelon the way other men picked up grapefruit. Faded, knee-sagging Levi's that once fit him like sausage casing now drooped from his bony hips. His nose had been an early loser in barroom brawls during his drifter years, when he fought at the drop of a hat. No one could plant a fist on him when he was sober, but that was almost never; by the time he finally settled down and ceased scrapping, the damage had been done. His nose rode like a smashed potato astride his hollow cheeks.

His one remaining eye glittered from beneath the wide-brimmed Stetson, a pale ghostly blue light almost totally rinsed of color.

He stood just inside the door, running a long forefinger beneath the black eye patch, and flicked out a warm bubble of sweat that had collected in the hollow of the empty left socket. Rumor had it he lost the eye fighting with Pancho Villa. In truth it had been knocked out of his head in a Mexican whorehouse by the satin-shoed toe of a high-kicking dancer.

At the sight of him, bank vice-president Billy Hale sprang

3

from behind the counter and scurried in a waddling run across the marble lobby, a short fat man with perilously high blood pressure and a jittery heart.

"Howdy, Witt!" he panted, smiling servilely, grabbing Witt's unoffered hand. "What can I do for you?"

"I've come to draw out all my money," Witt said.

Billy's pudgy hand turned to ice. His heavy cheeks flushed red, as if all his blood had suddenly shot upwards.

His color alarmed Witt. "Just joking, Billy. Don't go work yourself into a hissy." He pried his fingers from Billy's cold clasp.

"You darn near scared the pants off me," Billy said, resurrecting his smile. He pulled out his handkerchief and mopped his forehead. Losing the bank's biggest account would mean closing the doors.

"You should have known I was just pulling your leg, Billy. If I took out all that money, where in the world would I put it? I already got every bank in South Texas chock full of cash."

Billy was laboring for breath, trying to control the nervous twitch that had set his right eye to fluttering. "You shouldn't scare a man like that. The old ticker's pumping to beat the band." He patted his chest to illustrate.

Witt smiled easily. "My apologies, Billy. Matter of fact I just dropped by to have another look-see at my safety-deposit box."

Billy sighed with relief. "Sure thing, Witt. Come on in back. I'll fetch it for you."

Witt followed him, took the box in his hand, backed into Billy's private office mumbling, "Pardon me," and kicked the door shut with the toe of his boot.

The smile tumbled like a weight from Billy's lips. He stood facing the closed door, twisting his nose between his

4

fingers. He was dying to know what Witt had in that box. Like everyone else in Landry he had heard wild tales about a diamond. Every so often, especially when Witt called at the bank and holed up in back with the box, someone revived the old rumor and kicked it around again. The story went that Witt had picked up a fabulous diamond along with the Rolls-Royce he bought when old man Mendoza's estate was auctioned off in Brownsville before the war.

Everyone had seen the Rolls-Royce with its chrome-plated headlamps, shiny bright as new money, and two spare tires nestled into the front fenders. Witt didn't always drive into town in the cab of his jalopy pickup. On special occasions like fairs and funerals they caught sight of him in the big car sailing through the streets perched like a skipper, high in the leather seat with the enormous prow sticking out half a block in front of him. People stopped and pulled off the road as he glided past; car-chasing dogs, brought to bay by its size, whined and cowered against curbs; and boys of seven or eight, convinced it was Al Capone's getaway vehicle, dared each other as it paused for stop signs to fly into the street and give its license plate a good-luck slap.

The Rolls-Royce was real enough. But the diamond! It remained a tantalizing mystery.

Billy glowered resentfully at the door, wishing he had X-ray vision, willing to give a month's salary to see if the diamond was real. He backed away reluctantly and padded down the hallway to the bookkeeping office. He pulled the ledger from the shelf and leafed through the blue-lined pages until he came to Witt's account. His throat went dry as he read the balance: $4,178,701.19. Incredible!

He felt a warm reverent flush as his blood pressure rose in homage to all that money. A moaning sound of wonder erupted from his lips at the thought of similar amounts,

5

maybe even larger, that Witt had stashed away in other banks from there to the Rio Grande.

The bookkeeper looked up, startled by the odd noise issuing from Billy. "Mr. Hale, you don't look so hot!"

Billy teetered like a tightrope walker losing his balance. "I don't feel so hot."

His round, jowly face had gone a hideous purple. A jewel-like bubble of saliva twinkled brightly from the downturned corner of his parted lips. The moaning grew louder, rising to a growl.

"Mr. Hale!" the bookkeeper cried in alarm. She jumped from her chair and caught him as he pitched forward across the opened ledger book. He spun on a rubbery leg, then slumped sideways, crushing her with his weight before collapsing with a thud to the floor.

Albert Pugh, the loan officer, heard her cries and flew down the hall. He froze in the doorway aghast. Billy was gasping feebly, his face undergoing an astonishing change of color—from livid purple to red; then pink, and finally a gruesome chalky gray.

"Call an ambulance!" Albert cried, shoving the bookkeeper toward the phone. All the while awful things were going on in Billy's brain as blood rushed into places where it shouldn't have gone and ceased to flow into places where it should have. As Albert listened for a heartbeat, one billion tiny brain cells in Billy's head dried up and died.

The ambulance came and took Billy away before Witt reemerged. He found the lobby buzzing with gossipy excitement.

"What the hell happened? A holdup?"

Betty Jean Schneider, the stout head teller, wheeled around, tickled to be the first to break the news. "It's Billy Hale. He up and had a stroke, right in the bookkeeper's office."

"Is he dead?"

Betty Jean rolled her eyes to the ceiling. "He sure didn't look too alive to me."

Witt's eyebrows raised and his bottom lip protruded as if he had just heard a tall tale. "Hardly seems possible. . . . I was just talking to him a minute ago."

"It hit him quick as a wink. He was checking the ledger one minute and deader 'n a doornail the next. Makes you kinda think, don't it? I mean, how old was Billy? Couldn't have been fifty yet."

Witt nodded pensively. "I reckon that's a fair guess."

"Horrible thing to see," Betty Jean went on, "the poor thing lying there on the floor gray as a ghost and looking like this." She shut her eyes and dangled her tongue from the side of her mouth in imitation of Billy's agony.

Witt looked away in disgust. He stowed his safety-deposit box and fled through the door.

He stopped on the sidewalk, blinking in the sunlight. Roseanne had moved. She was now camped across the street directly opposite, keeping watch from behind pink-rimmed sunglasses. When she spotted him she finished lighting another cigarette from the glowing butt of the last, French-inhaled, and gave the horn a tentative toot.

Witt stared at her without responding. She was a hawk-faced woman, twenty years younger than he, small and wiry, with highly rouged cheeks and a beak-sharp nose cutting an inverted V above thin, very red lips. Her tinted auburn hair circled her head like a wreath of springy red fringe. Wrinkles, faint tracings of Witt's, cut across her forehead and etched lines over the hard angles of her cheeks.

Time was, Witt reminisced, when Roseanne was pretty, stringing along half the men in the county before she fell for Possom Woodley's glib line and fancy duds. He hadn't done much for her except fritter away her inheritance and make her even greedier than she was born.

Witt gave a snort halfway between distaste and pity. She reminded him of a spoiled kid who grabs the biggest piece of birthday cake and cries because the lucky dime was baked into the smallest.

Across the street Roseanne's finger was raised, beckoning him imperiously. He considered ignoring her again, but it had been six months since they last talked, and he sensed an opportunity to gain an inch or two in their tug-of-war.

Hitching his Levi's over his sharp hipbones he stepped off the curb and crossed the street to her car.

Her engine was idling like a motorbike trying to haul a trailer uphill. He waited for her to roll down the window. Instead she started shouting through the closed glass. "How do you like the new car Possom bought me?"

Witt cupped his hand behind his ear, pretending he couldn't hear.

Two thick cords swelled in Roseanne's neck as she hollered even louder. "I said, what do you think of my new Cadillac?"

Witt shrugged and made a circular motion with his fist for her to roll down the window.

Her mouth twitched with impatience. "I know goddamn well you can hear me."

Witt denied this with a headshake.

"Ha!" she shouted triumphantly. "You gave yourself away! You may be half blind but you're not deaf!"

Witt grinned, conceding her point.

"I got to keep the windows shut up tight so the cold air won't pour out. This is the first air-conditioned car in Landry, I'm tickled to say. Climb in and cool off a spell."

She watched him circle the car. Despite his age he moved like a bobcat, still smooth and silky.

He opened the door and slipped in beside her.

"Some fancy car, huh?" she said. Her chin jutted forward sharply, challenging him to deny it. "Sort of puts that old-fashioned locomotive of yours in the shade, don't you think?"

"I'm a jealous wreck," Witt replied.

Roseanne fiddled with the controls, increasing the rush of icy air. "This thing can blow cold as a Blue Norther."

"For all the noise it makes, it damn sure ought to."

Roseanne sat back suddenly, clamping two fingers over her nose. "P. U.! It must be hot as a firecracker out there. You smell like you just spent a month in a gopher hole."

Witt extended his arm so the cold airstream rushed up his sweaty sleeve.

"You're a disgrace to the famiy name, Witt Tyler, traipsing around in public dressed worse than a tramp and stinking to high heaven. A good dousing with Possom's eau de cologne wouldn't do you any harm."

"What do I want that crud for? There's nobody out at the ranch but me and the dog, and she never complained yet."

Roseanne wrinkled her nose even further, until it squashed between her cheeks. "People used to wonder why you never got yourself married. Bachelor, rich as Croesus, all alone on that empty ranch of yours! Lord have mercy, one whiff of you and it wouldn't take an Einstein to figure out why the ladies stayed away!"

Witt reared back, offended. "That's not true! I had myself plenty of chances. There was that girl at the university. . . ."

"You mean the dean's daughter, the one you got caught buck naked with in the bushes at Barton Springs?"

"Naturally you got the story all wrong."

"I'm only repeating what Seyton wrote home to Daddy."

"So that's how the old man found out? My own brother carrying tales home from school."

"Daddy had a right to know why you got expelled."

"No expelled about it. I left under my own steam. Anyway there were other women . . . like that fine Creole lady in New Orleans who took quite a fancy to me." His voice dropped to a fond purr. "I sure cut a dashing figure back then, before I lost my eye and got my nose busted up."

"The way I heard it she was married and her husband showed you the highway with the point of a gun."

Witt sneered. "That pantywaist. I offered to duel with him."

Roseanne guffawed. "And I guess you left a trail of broken-hearted señoritas all those years you spent hiding out from Daddy in Mexico?"

Witt nodded solemnly. "Any number of them. I remember one pretty little thing in particular. Kept begging me to marry her and take her to New York. She was an actress."

"Actress my hind foot! Is that what they call those women down there?"

Witt ignored the slur. He removed his Stetson and wiped the sweat from the headband. "She was an honest-to-god actress, Mexico's first motion-picture star."

Roseanne nodded knowingly. "I'm sure she was . . . and schoolboys are getting caught every day trying to smuggle those nasty movies across the Rio Grande."

She waited for Witt's parry but he was looking past her to the bank doors, where Betty Jean Schneider was taping up a large black-bordered notice.

"So Billy Hale is dead," she said. "I saw them cart him away in the ambulance. For a minute there I thought sure it was you."

"Disappointed?"

Roseanne merely shrugged. "It set me to wondering whether you ever got around to drawing up a will."

"I don't see how that concerns you."

10

She looked at him as if he had gone crazy. "It sure as hell better concern me! If you take off without a will, everything you own gets split up four ways among the three brothers and me. That's the law. That means I'm in line for nothing bigger than a quarter share."

She paused deliberately. "Can't you understand, Witt? I want it all. The others don't need another cent. Emmett's still holding onto his part of Daddy's ranch and got holdings in a couple of oil wells to boot. Seyton's been lining his pockets with a pretty penny ever since he got in cahoots with the judge."

Witt smirked. "Yeah, I heard the two of them were thick as thieves."

Roseanne gave him a wink, almost fondly. "That's pretty close to the mark. I hear Seyton skims off fifty per cent of every suit he wins in court, and the judge sees to it he wins a lot. No telling how much kickback he's taking home. So Seyton is sitting pretty. And Floyd's certainly set for life. The church gives him a house and all he can eat for climbing the pulpit every Sunday to bore the pants off the Methodists. That leaves me saddled with Possom, who goes broke every time the wind shifts."

Witt laughed at her. He had heard the tune before, the same complaints, the same badgering about his will. She was sure she was going to outlive him, and was determined to reap a profit out of her longevity.

He plopped his hat back on his head. "Roseanne, before I'd let you get your greedy hands on a penny of mine I'd give it all away to a Mexican orphan home."

She fired up another cigarette, letting the remark pass. He had threatened worse things.

"I should have kept better track of my philanderings," he went on, enjoying himself. "Somewhere along the line there's

11

bound to be a little bastard that looks like me. Yep, if he's out there I sure would like to find him. It would tickle me to pieces to cut your water off like that."

Roseanne pulled her sunglasses down her nose with her forefinger and fixed him with a hard stare over the pink rims. "I wouldn't count on any of your past mistakes turning up in bulrushes. And at your age I don't reckon there's likely to be any new ones."

"It's been done before."

"Yeah, I think I read about such a case once in *Believe It or Not*. Anyway it would have to be by long-distance telephone. No living, breathing woman could stand getting that close to you."

"There's still one or two."

Roseanne's hands flew up. "Well, Lordie, I don't want to hear about it! The very idea turns my stomach."

Witt grinned and slouched down in the seat. The cold air and the engine's drone were making him drowsy.

"What were you doing in the bank? Admiring that diamond you got stashed away inside?"

Witt peered at her suspiciously from beneath his brim. "What diamond are you talking about?"

"Come off it! Everybody and their dog knows you've got a diamond big as a walnut. Why don't you let me see it?"

"What do you want to see another diamond for? You got your hands on all of Mama's, more than you can wear at any one time."

"Shoot!" Roseanne scoffed. "Those little bitty things? I never saw so many chips in all my life."

Witt sat up and stared at her coldly. "I was supposed to get some of those little bitty chips, remember? Mama promised them to me the morning she died, the little Tiffany ring and the round brooch she always wore on Sunday. They should have come to me like Mama wanted."

Roseanne shrugged him off. "It's not my fault you acted the way you did, whoring, boozing it up, landing in jail so often that's where they sent your mail. Then disappearing in Mexico with a revolution going on until Daddy gave you up for dead."

"If he gave me up for dead, why'd he bother to cut me off with a single dollar?"

"As far as he was concerned, you were as good as dead. He didn't have the strength to worry about you after all you put him through."

"I don't suppose my conniving brothers whispering in his ear did much to change his mind." He sank back in the seat and shivered. "Can't you turn that machine down? I'm freezing my tail off."

"What's the use of having it if you don't feel the cold? Anyway, if you don't intend to show me your diamond I'm going to be shoveling off."

Witt reached for the door handle. "I don't have a goddamned thing to show you, Roseanne."

Her jaws were tight. She crushed her last cigarette into the overflowing ashtray. "I'll lay eyes on it one of these days. You can bet your boots on that."

Before getting out, Witt leaned across and offered his cheek. "How about a sisterly kiss?"

Roseanne cringed. "I'd rather kiss a horse's ass."

"That reminds me. Tell Possom 'hi'!" His pale eye flashed from the shadow of his hat.

Her back wheels shrieked as she shot away from the curb, making Witt jump back or be sideswiped. As she sailed around the corner ignoring the stoplight, he caught a last glimpse of her face, stony beneath the tight red fringe.

He crossed the street, read the posted notice of Billy Hale's death, and ambled back to the old jalopy pickup he had left in the billboard shade down the street.

He sat behind the wheel for a moment with the motor idling, trying to remember what was making him think he ought to go back home. Whatever it was had slipped his mind. Finally he gave up, abandoning the worrisome thought. He wrestled the ancient truck into the lower of its two remaining gears and bounced out into the street.

"I wonder if Katie's home," he thought. "I sure as hell would like to see Katie."

CHAPTER TWO

Katie McIntosh bleached her hair blond and told everybody she was "staring forty in the face"; "looking back at fifty" would have been more like it. She was a tall, square-shouldered widow with big bones, a blowsy complexion, and audacious, high-riding breasts whose freckled tops she flashed around town in low-cut dresses. Her legs were very good, as long as a man's, but with an eye-catching shapeliness she capitalized on by squeezing her big feet into four-inch heels that pumped her calves into their most seductive curves.

Her clothes could have come from the sheriff's auction of a bankrupt gypsy: a gaudy ragbag of sateen blouses, circular skirts, heavy lace, and massive gold-dipped bracelets that clanged together around her thick wrists like brassy temple bells.

She lived alone in a house called "the castle" by neighborhood children, a two-story gingerbread relic rushing headlong down the road to ruin. It stood forlorn and forbidding in the middle of a desolate, weedy yard. Its scaly walls sagged and buckled like wet cardboard. Its roof sank in on itself shedding shingles like dead leaves. A round tower rose out-of-plumb above the treetops and poked a lightning rod at the sky.

For days on end the big dark windows stayed tightly shut and curtained. The doors were latched. There was no sign of life—as if the house had turned its back on the world. Then unexpectedly it would be thrown open, the curtains swept back, the windows raised, the doors propped ajar while warm breezes filled the rooms.

All this was noted by the children who kept watch on the place, for they believed with bone-chilling certainty that "the castle" was haunted by the ghost of Katie's only child, Wally.

In 1945, in the last few weeks of the war, Katie got word that Wally had been killed on an island somewhere in the Pacific. She went into seclusion, barricading herself inside the house for nearly a month. At last, when she reappeared, people discovered to their horror that she refused to believe the news. She continued to write letters to the boy, to send him small packages of cigarettes and candy; and, because some of these letters and packages had never found their way back to her, she remained convinced that he was still alive and had received them. No one, not even Witt, could persuade her otherwise.

His old pickup kicked gravel in Katie's driveway and shuddered to a stop. He stomped up the back steps, pushing through the screen door without knocking.

"Katie!" he hollered.

She appeared at the top of the stairs wrapped in an orange and yellow flowered kimono, tied up at the waist with a plush fringed sash. She smiled when she saw him. Placing one hand flat against the small of her back and cocking her big hips forward, she began descending the steps. It was a gesture that Witt found bizarrely sexy.

"You dog!" she said as she reached the bottom. Witt watched her heavy breasts sway and settle beneath the shimmery cloth.

16

Her voice was deep as a man's, full of smoke and air. Her big bright teeth flashed through her smile. "Where in God's creation have you been hibernating? I haven't laid eyes on you since Christmas."

Witt was standing on the other side of the room holding his Stetson down around his knee. "Truth is I haven't been much of anywhere," he said. "Mostly hanging out at the ranch with the dog, watching the creeks rise."

"Now, that's where you country folk have it all over us city slickers. Imagine, whole seasons full of exciting doings like that!" She fired him a wink. "Let's have a beer and chew the fat. I've got a bone to pick with you."

"Sounds like you're inviting me to lunch."

Katie ignored him. She pulled two bottles of Southern Select out of the refrigerator and led him onto the screened-in porch.

She set Witt's beer on the arm of a sagging wicker chair and stretched out along the glider, sucking white foam from the bottle neck. "The point is," she said after smacking her lips, "whatever happened to that trip we were supposed to make to Mexico?"

Witt looked blank. "I must have forgot all about it."

"Well, I haven't, you one-eyed heartbreaker. I know you were drunk when you promised, but I'm damned if that'll get you off the hook."

"What in the world do you want to go to Mexico for?"

"Because I've lived in this godforsaken hole that calls itself a town for twenty-five years and I've never even seen the Rio Grande. Christ, it's only a hundred miles away! Might as well be on the moon!"

"You mean Mr. McIntosh never took you across?"

Katie was breathing on her fingernails and polishing them against the shiny fabric stretched tightly across her breasts. She held out her hand, examining the nails, and gave him a

17

confidential glance through her fingers. "He told me he'd been there once before. McIntosh never liked doing anything more than once. I can verify that!"

Witt laughed, tilting back his head until he was staring into the ceiling fan set spinning by the lazy breeze. "Lordie, I reckon I spent more than enough time in old May-hee-co, and believe me, Katie, I didn't lose a goddamn thing down there."

"Easy for you to say, but I want to see it for myself. I'm longing to cross that border and really hang one on, have myself a big toot for a change. I want to drink tequila sours in those nightclubs and watch the *putas* do it with donkeys."

Witt sat upright, scandalized. "That's a story, Katie! That's not true!"

"Like hell you say! I've heard it from too many people for it to be a lie." She stopped swinging in the glider and studied his face. "What the hell are you smiling at?"

Witt broke into a broad grin. "You're an old bawd, Katie."

She scoffed. "It takes guts for a man your age to call someone else old."

"I'm younger than I look."

"Good Lord, Witt, you'd *have* to be!"

He crossed his legs and hung his Stetson on the toe of his boot. "Go on, guess how old I am."

"I *know* how old you are. But you look a hundred, and I'm fudging a little because we're good friends." She took a gulp of beer and swilled the bottle around to show him he was lagging behind. "Come on, old-timer, you're slowing down. Used to be you could pack away two of these to my one."

But Witt passed up her challenge. He was staring beyond her. His vacant, expressionless face caused her to sit up with concern. "What's the matter, Witt?"

He didn't answer but said instead: "Do I really look that old, Katie?"

She smiled softly and sank back into the glider, nudging it into motion. "Oh, Witt, I was just needling you. Don't get your feelings hurt by my going-on."

But Witt wasn't convinced by her tone. "I've been thinking about having a checkup," he said suddenly, surprising himself because he had been thinking no such thing. But the idea took hold. "You know, just to see if everything is still in working order." He looked at Katie to measure her reaction. Going to a doctor when he felt perfectly well seemed startlingly novel to him.

Katie was nodding dreamily. "People do it all the time . . . not me though. I'm a scaredy-cat. If there's something gnawing away at my insides I don't want to know about it. When I'm feeling down I just drop in on the chiropractor and have my back popped. That always does the trick . . . besides"— and she gave him a lewd wink—"I like his hands on me."

"Goddamn, Katie!"

She laughed and shifted her big feet on the porch. "Well, amigo, what's on the menu? Shall I get dressed or undressed?"

Witt shook his head, looking almost sad. "Might as well get dressed, Katie, cause I'm taking off. I better get me a seat in Dr. Koury's waiting room."

She moved behind him and rubbed his shoulders with her strong hands. He seemed to settle beneath her touch.

"There's nothing wrong with you, Witt," she said. "You're just lonesome and bored."

"I've never been bored a day in my life."

"Lonesome?"

He shrugged. "I don't know. Maybe so. . . . When you've lived alone as long as I have something like that gets hard to tell."

19

She closed her eyes wistfully. "Go see your doctor, Witt. . . ."

Witt sat perched awkwardly on the edge of the paper-covered table, his long legs dangling to the floor, as Dr. Michael Koury pulled at his eyelid and peered into the blue-white iris. Throughout the examination Witt had kept up a nervous one-way patter, stopping only to respond to the young doctor's questions. Inevitably the talk turned to the oil business.

"Hell, Doc, I still don't know any more about sands and cores than I did back in 'thirty-three, when the geologists from Beaumont brought in our first wildcat. All I know is wherever they sink pipe on my place more oil gushes out. I don't ask how, I just say, 'Thank you kindly,' and mail the checks to the bank."

Koury shifted to the side and looked through his otoscope into Witt's ear. "Ever get a duster?"

"Must have had one or two, but for the life of me I can't remember. Mostly just good, productive wells. That's a funny thing, too, because there've been a whole passel of dry holes on Herman Brandt's farm just the other side of my spread. Poor old Herman! From time to time I catch sight of him riding that smoke-farting tractor of his, looking over at my place with greedy eyes, wishing to high heaven his property line was located half a mile farther south."

Koury smiled. "How did you come into that ranch anyway? I heard . . ."

Witt nodded. He looked over the doctor's shoulder, peering through the blank wall into the past. "Just luck, I guess, pure-dee luck. I'd been fooling around in Mexico for any number of years when I suddenly came down with the strongest case of homesickness anybody ever had. I don't rightly know why such a thing came over me, I'd been on my own for so long. But there it was, this longing feeling to come back to Landry and see my folks again. So I took a boat out of Veracruz, happy as a coot to be coming home at last."

He stopped for a moment, seeing it all again. "Well, I got the shock of my life. I walked up to the old ranch house and found out my Daddy was dead going on a year. What's more, I'd been cut out of the inheritance. Received the grand sum of one dollar, to be exact. Everything else went to my brothers and Roseanne."

"Stand up and cough," Koury said.

Witt coughed perfunctorily and climbed back on the table. "Then came a long stretch of years when I was nothing better than a bum, you might say; everybody else did. I picked cotton alongside the Mexicans and wrangled for a couple of ranchers down around Benavides. Then my aunt Frieda got kicked in the head by her Tennessee Walker. Blow killed the old girl outright. When they read her will they found she left her entire ranch to me."

He chuckled. "You know what that will said? I memorized it word for word, cause it was short enough and kind of funny. It said: 'I leave all my earthly possessions to my nephew, Witt Tyler. I never liked the rest of the family, but I always liked Witt okay—at least what I saw of him, which wasn't much, thank the Lord.'"

Koury sat back on his stool and laughed out loud.

"Honest to God, Doc! That's what the old lady wrote!"

"So you became a rancher."

"Yeah, in a half-assed sort of way. It sure relieved my mind when we struck oil. I haven't worked the place a day since."

Witt eased his feet to the floor and reached for his Levi's. He took a deep breath. "Well, Doc, what's the story?"

Koury answered as he scribbled across a prescription pad.

"Not too bad for a man your age. Your blood pressure is too high, but this medicine ought to keep it in check."

Witt sighed with relief.

"Just take things easy."

"Hell, Doc, if I took things any easier I'd have to stay in bed. I've already buried three doctors in this town and I aim to outlast you."

Koury smiled, passing him the prescription. "If crowds like that in the waiting room keep up, I wouldn't be a bit surprised if you did."

Witt donned his Stetson and reached for the door. He turned and lowered his voice. "Did you see Billy Hale this morning?"

Koury nodded. "He was DOA at the hospital."

"What got him, Doc?"

Koury made a pistol out of his hand and fired it at his temple. "A stroke. Pow! He never knew what hit him."

Witt grimaced. "Goddamn, you really know you're old when the younger ones start dying off around you."

"Take care of yourself and you'll stick around for a long time yet."

"I intend to, Doc. I'm not ready to feed the worms, not by a long goddamned shot."

He stepped outside into the bright afternoon sun and scanned the sky. It had crowded with blue-bellied anvil clouds. From far in the distance, rolling in across the flat plains, came the rumble of thunder. He hurried across the street and climbed into his pickup.

"Well, look who's back," Katie said. She had changed into what she called her "Carmen Miranda outfit," a ruffled skirt of blinding pink with a white lace peasant blouse she wore well down off the shoulders.

22

Witt stood just inside the kitchen door, his hat in one hand and two bottles of champagne, bought chilled, hanging like juggler pins from the other. "I came back to celebrate," he announced. "*El doctor* says I'm fit as a fiddle."

"What's that you've got there . . . two bottles of fancy beer?"

"Poor Katie." He shook his head in mock pity and set the champagne on the table. "Don't you know nothin'? This here is French shampoo."

He tore at the silver foil, but Katie interrupted him with: "Let's wait, Witt. Stow it in the icebox and we'll drink it afterwards." Her voice was very quiet.

Witt looked up. In the dim light of the approaching storm he could see that she had not moved from the doorway, but she had pulled the blouse down around her waist, covering her breasts with her hands. Witt put the bottles away and crossed the kitchen to wind his arms around her.

"Witt . . ." Katie began. Her eyes dropped but there was a smile on her lips. ". . . take a bath first."

"Whoopee!" shouted Witt as the cork from the second bottle ricocheted off the ceiling and exploded into an open box of Katie's white body powder.

They were snuggled deep in Katie's four-poster sipping champagne between bites of tortillas and butter. Intermittent flashes of lightning touched the darkened walls with silver. The streaming square window panes rattled against the wild thunder. Rain stung the house like flying sand. Their heads were framed like oval daguerreotypes in the parchment light from Katie's two bedside lamps.

"I'm three sheets to the wind," giggled Katie.

"I'm four."

"I'm *five!*" She rolled over, nestling close to him, and

offered her jelly glass to be refilled. A drop splashed onto her forearm and he took the sparkling bubble with the tip of his tongue.

Katie said, "There's nothing wrong with us that a little loving and a lot of champagne won't cure."

"Damn right, and you got to have both, only I'd like lots of each."

"How come you never married, Witt?"

He shrugged casually. "I don't know. I never found the right one I guess. Maybe one of these days I'll marry you."

"The hell you will! I'm not going to make the same mistake twice."

"How's that?"

"Marrying a man who won't take me to Mexico."

Witt laughed. "I'm going to take you, Katie. I promise."

She smiled at him and sat up reaching for her kimono. "I'm dying to see Mexico. I don't want to spend the rest of my life holed up in Landry. You know, I'm really a city girl. Chicago born and Chicago bred. It's funny, Witt, I probably would have stayed there forever if I hadn't married McIntosh. I was crazy in love with him, I thought. He was such a helluva lot of fun. Big show . . . big show, full of talk and fancy dreams. And what happens? We end up in Landry, Texas. Jesus H.! I didn't even know they made towns as little as this. I wasn't here five minutes before I started to hold it against him. I'd wake up every morning with the hot sun in my eyes thinking I would pack my bags, take a taxi to the depot, and buy a ticket back home. Then the next thing I'd know it'd be nighttime and the train north had already left.

"After I had Wally, I kept thinking: I'm going to get us out of here before he starts school. And then, before he gets into high school. But I never did. All of a sudden McIntosh caught pneumonia for the third time and died. That was sort of funny, too, because even after we put him in the ground, I kept right on thinking that one of these days I'll pack up and leave him . . . just like he was still around. I guess he sort of beat me to the punch . . . though I'm not sure I'd want to go where he was headed." She paused wistfully and took a sip of champagne. Her tone brightened.

"We're two old-timers now, Witt. You know that? Everybody's dying off all around us and we're being left behind."

"Like King of the Mountain," Witt said.

"King and Queen of the Mountain." She giggled and suppressed a belch with the back of her hand. "Come on, Witt, let's make a list. Let's start with Fannin Street and name off all those people who've slipped off the mountain."

"Jerry Waters," Witt said, falling in with the game.

"Right. First house on Fannin."

"Then Maydee Lou Williams."

"And Felix Williams and Frank Tibbets."

"You skipped a house. Before Tibbets there was Ellen Magee."

"Forgot about her."

"Then Doris and Henry Daspit, and Henry Jacobs and Louis Newman."

"And Louis's first wife, whatchamacallit."

"We're only up to Guadalupe Street," Witt said softly. "Poor things."

"Do you figure they were ready, Katie?"

She shrugged. "Maybe. Some people get tired quicker than others."

"I'm not tired, by God. There's still a lot of things I want to do."

"Me, too."

25

"Why are you hanging around here, Katie? Why don't you do what you said, pack up and catch the train north?"

She sighed and stood up, wrapping the kimono around her. "Maybe I will one of these days. Maybe I will when Wally gets back. . . ."

Witt grew somber. "Oh, Katie. He's dead. You know it in your heart. After all this time he's not going to be coming back." He kept his voice low, trying to be gentle.

Katie looked out the window as the last few drops splashed against the panes and the clouds pulled apart into patches of turquoise light. "I'm not going to believe that until I see his body with my own eyes."

From the dresser top she took a letter she received from the Army a week before and handed it to Witt. "They're sending a casket home in a couple of weeks. I intend to have a look inside."

Witt shuddered. "You don't want to do that."

Katie opened the window to the warm air made moist and heavy by the storm. "I have a feeling, Witt, just one of those premonitions. I think Wally's still alive out there somewhere and that he's going to be coming back. I think I'll just hang around here for a little while longer and wait. If it's true, and if he does come back, then maybe we'll head for Chicago."

Witt threw the letter on the pillow and grabbed for his clothes. "I'm tired of this talk, Katie. The whole day's been full of death."

She was staring out the window at the silvery pools of rainwater flashing in the light of the newly emerging sun. "I had a good time, Witt. It was a great way to pass a storm."

Witt didn't reply. The mood was crushed between them. He hurried downstairs and left the house weary with depression.

She watched from the window until the pickup disappeared down the driveway. Then, picking up the letter from the pillow, she descended the stairs. Dry words, dry eyes. She carried it to the kitchen and set fire to it in the sink. The paper writhed in the yellow flames. The ashes clotted against the wet white porcelain.

She stared at the soggy, black shapes, trying to read them as if they were tea leaves in a china cup. Finally she flushed the sink with water and guided the ashes into the drain.

When she finished she went about the house drawing the curtains against the afternoon light. The neighborhood children who had been spying on the house noted this with quickening hearts. They knew what it meant. The ghost was coming back.

On the highway home Witt was again nagged by the feeling that something needed tending to, of something left undone. When he pulled up in the yard outside his house he smelled smoke. He jumped from the truck thinking his house was on fire. The pickup's door swung wide in the whistling wind that sailed through the opposite window and lifted the unfilled prescription from the seat. It flew across the yard, tumbling over clumps of dry grass, and snagged along with other tattered debris on the barbed wire fence.

With his hat fanning a path through the blue smoke Witt fumbled his way to the kitchen. Only then did he remember the frijoles he left to simmer. He threw open a window and hurled the scorched pot into the yard. The stench permeated the house. It lingered all day.

As the sun went down he set his radio in the window and stretched out in the hammock on the back porch. His old dog, Minnie, scratched up the steps and curled up beneath the hammock. Witt reached down and patted her scruffy rump.

27

The hammock rocked gently in the evening breeze floating in from the distant Gulf.

He stared out over his land: the brief twilight softened the empty, unmarked horizon, now totally cloudless, washed clean by the rain. Nothing broke the immense flatness that spread forth unrelieved as far as he could see.

"You'd never know a storm passed this way," he mumbled to the dog. "If you'd slept all day and just now opened your eyes, you'd never believe there'd been a big rain. God, it's just like some of us. We move on past and leave nothing behind."

Darkness crawled across the sky, a deep awesome lonely cover. The stars came out, first one by one and then by the hundreds, unwinking in the night air.

Witt shut his eye and fell asleep, lulled and kept company by the sighs of the nearby oil pumps breathing in his ear.

CHAPTER THREE

On the other side of the county in a three-room shack on E. B. Orville's farm lived the Sanchez family. Hector Sanchez was Mr. Orville's hand, hired for field work, plowing, sowing, chopping, and fencing; his wife, Carmen, swept, mopped, dusted, ironed, and washed dishes for Mrs. Orville. Their joint labors earned them fifteen dollars a week plus a corner nook in the vegetable garden and a sporadic donation of hand-me-down clothing whenever Mrs. Orville took a notion to clean out her closets.

She was also good about passing on to the Sanchez family the gristly remains of the Sunday roast on Tuesday or making them a gift of a pound of ground round suspected of having turned. On the latter occasions, Mrs. Orville was of two minds: first, apprehension that one or all of the Sanchezes would come down with ptomaine, leaving her with the annoyance of a "passel of sick Mexicans" on her hands, and second, when they had digested the chancy meat and continued to thrive, self-punishing resentment that she had given away food that was, after all, still good.

Thus housed, clothed, and fed, the Sanchezes were comfortably taken care of, as Mrs. Orville liked to think.

Lately, however, Hector Sanchez had begun to think otherwise. On twilight evenings sitting on the stoop of his little shack, as much curling tar paper as wood, sipping his daily beer, he pondered the situation. It was the beer, the one bottle a day, that started him thinking. There were times when he would have liked two or even three to wash his throat clean of the sand from a hot afternoon's plowing and a pouch of Bull Durham to go along with the beer whenever he felt the urge to smoke. But with six children and a wife, no matter how he cut it, fifteen dollars a week didn't go far.

The solution dawned on him as he drained his bottle and watched his eldest daughter, Noelia, ready the younger children for bed. At seventeen it was time she married and moved out from under his wing. One less mouth to feed would make all the difference. She was a fetching beauty with lustrous skin transparently olive and a strong young figure. Her hair, uncut since she was fourteen—the last year her mother had bothered to send her to school—fell in glossy black waves well past the center of her back. The irises of her dark-fringed eyes reflected light like polished mahogany. Her brow was smooth, her nose proudly arched, her pink lips curved in the provocative fullness of a pout. A husband would be easy to find.

Hector announced his decision along with the name of a likely prospect, a distant cousin, a boy Noelia had once seen at a family funeral.

The girl's eyes filled with tears. She knew intuitively about boys like that: their eyes roved while their wives swelled with pregnancy and worked as maids from dawn to dusk in the Anglo houses in town. She appealed to her mother for support, but Carmen looked away with flat eyes, siding with Hector.

Lying in her bed that night she prayed to the Virgin for help. She wasn't opposed to marriage; indeed she longed for the escape it promised; but not to a callow boy who would take her from her father's shack only to house her in another

30

exactly like it with a life of hard work ahead and money only for dried frijoles and tortillas. Instead, she wanted to be taken away by *un Señor,* a somebody, who would give her a house like Mrs. Orville's, with bright sweet-smelling rooms; curtained windows that slid up and down, electric lights, and most of all—because it was pure luxury—an indoor toilet. She had sneaked a use of the Orvilles' bathroom once, though Mrs. Orville, had she known about it, would have scrubbed the fixtures with Lysol. She had slipped in and out of the clean white room so quickly that no one ever suspected; but for one blissful minute she believed she knew what true comfort was.

She rolled over, kneading out a lump in the corn husk mattress and made a last appeal to the Virgin. "Please," she whispered aloud, taking no chance her prayer would go un-heard, "make me a miracle."

The next day the Virgin obliged.

In the hard dirt barnyard about halfway between the Orvilles' house and the Sanchezes' shack stood a rickety wooden windmill that creaked and spun in the breeze, pumping up salty water for use on the farm. There, in the angles of the windmill's legs, the Virgin chose to appear in a vision to the girl.

It happened a few moments before sunset. Hector had not yet trudged home from the fields, Carmen was waxing floors for Mrs. Orville, and the younger children were playing noisily among the chili plants that sprouted beside the little house.

Noelia had been stirring a pot of red rice on the smoky wood stove when she paused for a moment to brush her hair out of her eyes. In passing she glanced out the window in the direction of the windmill.

Something caught her attention and she laid down the spoon.

31

Initially there was only a dull awareness of a special atmosphere like rising heat in the stillness before a summer storm; then she heard music, at first subliminally faint, then growing louder, the sound of a thousand tinkling bells that seemed to rain out of the clear sky. Suddenly her eyes were dazzled by a glowing ball of light that hovered like an iridescent soap bubble above the windmill's silhouetted spire.

Noelia's heart pounded, seemingly crowding into her slender throat. She glided from the house as if her body had become weightless.

As she approached, the bells rang more loudly. The blinding aureole reached out for her, burning against her skin like slivers of ice, taking hold of her arms and legs, drawing her closer. Without warning, the shimmery bubble burst open, flaring outward into an oval ring of crackling flame, revealing at its center a lady, more beautiful than any Noelia had ever seen.

She stood with her hands folded over her breast, clothed in a long, flowing dress spun of blazing white diamonds. On her exquisite head was posed a tiny jeweled crown of gleaming gold.

Captivated by her beauty, Noelia reached out to touch the dazzling hem. At once the lady extended her arms, palms outward, fending her off. Noelia fell back as though struck by forked lightning. She dropped to her knees, waiting breathlessly for the lady to make known her intentions.

The lady opened her lips. Her voice rang more musically than the bells. She spoke in Spanish:

—I am the Lady of the Windmill, the Daughter of God, the Bride of the Holy Spirit, the Mother of our Lord Jesus Christ.

Noelia crossed her burning forehead, her lips, and her heart. Hot tears sprang from her eyes.

—I promised love and peace to those who visit this sacred spot. Those who are sick will find health in the holy waters of this blessed ground.

Noelia cried out with joy: *"María Santísima, Madre de Dios!"*

The Lady brought her forefinger to her pretty lips to silence Noelia before continuing.

—Spread my message, Noelia, servant of the Lord, and your fervent prayer shall be answered!

The ringing of the heavenly bells crashed around Noelia's astonished ears. Her hands flew to her open mouth to stifle a cry of ecstasy.

Then the Lady extended her long, lovely arms, fanning out the glittering folds of her garment, revealing within a lining of the deepest blue silk studded with twinkling stars. Rays of light streamed from her palms and burned like fire into Noelia's heart. The girl fell over in a stupor.

When she recovered, the Lady was gone.

She picked herself off the ground, trembling with fright that she had been struck blind by the vision. Gradually she realized that it had only grown dark. The ringing persisted as echoes in her ears. Her eyes stung with the beauty and light they had absorbed. She stumbled through the evening shadows to the little shack, her heart pumping wildly in her chest.

Hector was still absent, Carmen had not yet returned, and the children continued their noisy game in the yellow rectangle of lantern light that spilled through the doorway. Noelia splashed cold water against her face to calm her rapid breath and sank heavily into a chair.

When Carmen came in from the Orvilles' she found her daughter sitting immobile, pale and entranced. A thin blue rope of smoke wound its way upward from the pot on the stove.

33

"Aaaiiii!" she screamed, taking in the scene. *"Mira, idiota!* You've let the rice burn! Now we will be hungry!" She gave the still dazed girl a rough swipe alongside the head.

Fresh tears welled up in Noelia's eyes, but she kept from crying out. The other children abandoned their game and pressed their noses against the screen. Noelia ignored their spiteful giggles. The nuns had long ago taught her that people who saw visions were often abused, especially by their own family.

Carmen threw open the door, scattering the children, and flung the burned rice into the yard for the chickens. The blackened pot clattered into the wash tub. *"Idiota, imbécil, tonta!* she ranted, until she noticed the glassy cast in Noelia's eyes. A suspicious frown creased her forehead. She bent over her daughter and asked, "What's the matter with you? Are you sick?"

Noelia shook her head, not caring that her brothers and sisters were mocking her from the screen. *"Mamacita,* I have just seen the most beautiful lady. . . ."

Carmen listened intently to Noelia's story, silencing the children's snickers with the back of her hand. When Noelia finished, Carmen crossed herself three times. She did not doubt her daughter's word for a moment.

"Tomorrow, when it is light, take me to the windmill and show me where you saw the lady."

Noelia nodded. *"Sí,* Mama."

Carmen could not sleep. When the first turquoise glow of dawn brightened the horizon she roused her drowsy daughter by hissing in her ear. "Show me!"

Noelia led her mother across the silent yard and pointed to the windmill, which was catching the first rays of the rising sun.

"There, Mama, there!"

"*Aiiii!*" Carmen screamed, and sank to her knees, making the sign of the cross with furious speed. "I see it! I see it!"

"Mama!" Noelia cried. Her eyes scanned the windmill. "What do you see?"

"The image of the Lady! There . . . in the wood!"

"*Where?*" Noelia's shrill voice split the still morning air.

"Are you blind?" cried Carmen, pointing to one of the wooden braces that sloped down the windmill's right side. "Can't you see the image the Lady left behind?"

"But, Mama," Noelia protested, "she didn't appear there. It was lower down and on the other side."

"I see what I see," Carmen insisted. "Look!"

Noelia's eyes searched out the spot pointed to by her mother and came to rest on a vague discoloration in the wood that might have been etched into the grain by years of dripping water. It was a brownish parabola enclosing a darker area at the focus which looked like a knot in the wood but which, after Noelia had stared at it for a moment, could just as easily have been the image of the Lady's head beneath her flowing veil.

Hector, aroused by his wife's excited cries, joined the two women in the yard.

"Look!" shouted Carmen. "The image of the Virgin!"

The lights snapped on in the big house and Mr. and Mrs. Orville, still dressed in their nightclothes, straggled into the yard to investigate the commotion.

"Look!" Carmen said to them when they approached. "The Virgin has appeared to Noelia. Can you see her image on the windmill?"

The Orvilles looked first to the windmill, then at each other. "Shoot!" said Mr. Orville unimpressed. Without another word they re-entered their house, where Mrs. Orville began spooning coffee into her percolator.

Mr. Orville reappeared in the kitchen and sat down at the table to pull on his boots. "It sure don't take much to get a Mexican all worked up. Excitable lot. . . ."

Mrs. Orville struck a match and lit the gas on a rear burner. They were hard-shell Southern Baptists and didn't believe in visions.

"Shoot," said Mr. Orville, shaking his head in wonder and amusement. "That ol' water stain has been there for a hunnerd years."

Hector squinted at the windmill for a long time. Finally he spoke: "Get up, Carmen. Come back into the house."

Carmen remained on her knees, clapping her hands together as if she were patting tortillas. "I must take Noelia to Landry. She has to tell the story of the miracle to Father Anselmo."

A scowl darkened Hector's face. "No one will go to Landry. I forbid you to speak of this to anyone . . . even Father Anselmo." His eyes returned to the windmill. "No one will believe such a story. It will only make trouble."

Carmen opened her mouth to protest but thought better of it. Noelia merely sighed stoically, recalling what the sisters had taught her: the fathers of children who saw visions were often the hardest to convince.

"Remember what I said," continued Hector. With a hand on her elbow, he steered his wife back to their house, scattering the cackling chickens, who were pecking the rice they had just found. "You're to tell no one. I don't want any trouble."

Carmen's mouth pressed into a thin line of resentment. Noelia, following behind, nodded obediently. But in her mind, she uttered a swift prayer to the Lady of the Windmill, begging her to soften her father's heart.

Her parents disappeared inside, but Noelia lingered on the doorstep, regarding the shack, its gaping windows, the unpainted boards and tar paper patches. She was swept by a wave of emotion, approaching nostalgia, for the place—she was not destined to remain there much longer. A *Señor* was coming for her, to take her away. The Lady had promised. . . .

She turned her shining face to the rising sun and whispered a prayer of thanks.

CHAPTER FOUR

In or out of the money, Possom Woodley looked prosperous. Even during the lean years, when one get-rich scheme after another fell apart under his management, making Roseanne sell off her share of her father's ranch at depression prices to snatch him from the jaws of bankruptcy, he had been considered Landry's fanciest dresser: French cuffs, Italian silk ties, an alligator belt that matched his tasseled shoes, and the William Powell pose he affected in his red velvet smoking jacket whenever company dropped in. He modestly parried remarks about the ornate crest sewn over the breast pocket —a little too modestly, he hoped, in order to plant a lingering suspicion that he just might have title to the ornament after all.

Newcomers to Landry were bowled over by his erudition. "That Possom Woodley," they would say after an evening of drinking his expensive liquor. "He can talk on just about everything!" Old-timers, who knew him better, smirked back knowingly: "He's just a fool who reads the *Reader's Digest* from cover to cover."

Just before the war, Possom bought the creamery. To listen to him talk, Elsie the Cow had met her match. Six months later the business slipped through his fingers before charges of knowingly selling tainted milk. Brother-in-law Seyton saved him in court. It fell to brother-in-law Emmett to save him outside: at the time Emmett was dickering with some independent wildcatters for drilling rights on his ranch. At the last minute, to put an end to Roseanne's shrill badgering, Emmett extracted a gentleman's agreement from them that they buy their drill pipe from Possom.

It didn't faze Possom that he didn't have a foot of pipe to sell. On the strength of the order he marched into the now defunct Landry Bank & Trust and nailed down a loan from the feebleminded J. Willard Holland.

Possom sallied away with the money, bought the pipe, and immediately resold it to the oil men, using the profit to lease a dilapidated warehouse near the Tex-Mex Railroad tracks. From the beginning he was off and running, grabbing an order for a large amount of pipe, hustling down to the agreeable Mr. Holland for another loan, then scouring the area for the precious merchandise made scarce by the war. The orders poured in, for, as the oilmen often remarked: "Ol' Possom can get you all the pipe you want whether he has to beg, borrow, or steal." They were accurate on all three counts.

True to form, Possom's bubble finally burst. But this time it wasn't his fault. His old standby, the Landry Bank & Trust, closed its doors and went under as a direct result of the kindhearted overgenerosity and unwisdom of J. Willard Holland. For the first time since embarking on the pipe trade, Possom was having to seek a loan from the more cautious First State Bank. He found himself sitting on the other side of the desk facing Albert Pugh, whose dry lips were compressed even more tightly than usual.

Albert's silence and stern demeanor unnerved Possom and he launched again into a glib explanation of his latest deal.

39

As he listened, Albert appraised Possom with his cold thorough stare. His steely eyes lingered over the gaudy topaz cuff links, the matching pin that pierced the carefully dimpled tie, and the suspicious shine on Possom's manicured fingernails; and he didn't like what he saw. He looked up, thinking a man who got himself up like that has got to be part thief.

Possom matched him eyeball to eyeball: "I'm telling you, Albert, there ain't no risk involved at all. It's a lead-pipe cinch, if you'll pardon the expression."

Albert suppressed a wince and passed his hand over his lips. "I'm only concerned over your past record of business failures, Possom."

Possom wanted to spit in his face. Instead he flashed a winning smile. It never failed before. "Hell, man, that's ancient history . . . before I hit my stride. Look at me now. I got more business than I can take care of, fighting them off with a bat. If old J. Willard Holland had more customers like me, his bank would have been the biggest in the state."

Albert was unmoved. "That's a moot point, but the failure of the Landry Bank and Trust only proves that a man in my position can't be too careful." What he really meant was that with Billy Hale dead only a week, leaving the vice-presidency slot to be filled, he couldn't afford a mistake if he wanted the step up.

Possom began to sweat profusely. He shoved the order blank under Albert's nose. "Look at this thing, Albert. That's a helluva lot of pipe, three jobs worth. I got to have that loan to be able to deliver. I got a reputation to uphold. Those drillers trust me and I never welshed yet." What he didn't say, but what frightened him, was that the oilmen couldn't afford an idle rig. They were bound to haul him into court.

Albert considered Billy Hale's vacant desk out of the corner of his eye. He grew more recalcitrant. "This isn't a light decision to make, Possom. You understand that, of course. I'd like to talk it over with the other officers. It'll take a little time."

Time! The only thing besides ready cash Possom didn't have. His nervousness betrayed him. He leaped from his chair and snatched the order blank off the desk. "There're other banks, Albert, lots of them right here in Zamora County that got sense enough to spot a money-making deal when it hits them flat dab in the face. I just thought you people would appreciate the business. Maybe I'd better go shopping elsewhere."

Albert rose, extending his dry, pale hand. "That's probably not a bad idea, Possom, not a bad idea at all."

Possom left the bank choking on his beautifully knotted tie. When he reached his car he tore open his collar and panted for breath. It had never occurred to him that Albert would actually deny him the loan. That could pull down his whole house of cards.

He headed into a service station and ordered a tankful of gas. He had the uneasy feeling he was going to have to canvass every bank in Zamora County before the day was over. As he drove away, he doubled back around the block, cautiously avoiding the Cadillac showroom. He had promised he would be in that afternoon with the cash for Roseanne's new car.

A knock on the sacristy door at San Pablo's Catholic Church brought an impatient cluck to Father Anselmo's lips. He stretched a purple satin ribbon across the page he had been reading and closed his breviary with a snap. How could Holy Mother Church expect a priest to recite the Divine Office daily when he had to put up with a succession of trivial interruptions? Four in the past half hour alone!

Carmen Sanchez waited on the other side of the door, her massive head veiled in a black mantilla, her hand clasped tightly around Noelia's wrist. They had managed to slip away from the farm while Hector worked the fields. Carmen's brother, summoned from town, had driven them to the church. He now waited, drowsing behind the wheel, as Father Anselmo opened the door to the two women.

"Well?" he demanded. "Why have you knocked?"

Carmen found her tongue with difficulty. "Pardon me, Father. It's my daughter." She pointed to Noelia, who was hiding her head. "There has been a miracle. . . . The Mother of God has appeared to her. . . ."

In the sacristy, seated in his favorite chair with his forehead buried in his palm as if he were hearing confession, Father Anselmo listened to Noelia's story. He didn't believe a word of it. It was trite, a melodramatic hodgepodge of the fanciful stories spun by the sisters in catechism class. He could pick the various details apart and assign them one by one to their proper place in authenticated visions of the past. What a poor imagination this little peasant has, he thought as Noelia's words tumbled out, describing the oval aura which had blossomed into tongues of flame. Father Anselmo nodded. He was thinking: "Of course, she would have to include some detail stolen from the vision at Guadalupe. I'm only surprised she found room to work in aspects of Fátima and Lourdes."

He caught himself on the verge of laughing out loud. Rays from the lady's hands! Stars in her robe! Our Lady of the Windmill! Absurd!

Then Carmen said: "The Lady left her image behind."

Father Anselmo was so startled that his elbow slipped off the chair. His head snapped forward as if it had dislodged from his shoulders. When he recovered he asked, "What do you mean?"

Carmen drew herself up, realizing she had the priest in her hands. "After she left, the Lady put her image on the windmill. It's not large, but without doubt it is the Lady."

Father Anselmo sputtered. "There is, of course, some mistake. I mean, the image is no longer there, is it? It disappeared in time just like the vision, isn't that true?"

Carmen shook her large, square head. "You can still see it, Father, as plain as day."

Father Anselmo's face grew pale. He had been thinking this was simply a case of teen-age hysteria brought on by sexual frustration, mere adolescent fantasies. He expected to counsel the girl, chat with her mother, and leave the matter to settle later. Then, after a year, perhaps, he would officiate the marriage of the girl and she would see no more visions. That is how he handled cases like that in the past, simple problems, nothing new—but now the Sanchez woman had added a portentous twist.

"You are sure it is an image?" he murmured at last.

"Like our Lord's on the veil of Veronica," Carmen explained. She rather enjoyed instructing the priest.

"I must see it then," said Father Anselmo. "If this is true, then it is a miracle and I will have to inform the bishop."

Carmen relaxed in her chair. If the priest was coming to see it, he must believe. Suddenly another thought crossed her mind and she sat forward. "Come while my husband is away at work. He told us not to tell anyone. He is afraid of trouble."

Father Anselmo nodded sympathetically. Trouble, he thought, there'll be trouble all right if the news leaked out before he had time to write the bishop. "I will drive out to the farm as soon as I can. Until then, obey your husband, don't speak of this to anyone. And say the rosary three times daily as a precaution—in case this is a trick of the devil."

"Eeeeh!" went Carmen, sucking in her breath, covering her mouth; but Noelia sat up straight. "It couldn't be the devil. The Lady was too beautiful."

Carmen sighed with relief, comforted by Noelia's confidence.

Father Anselmo felt no such comfort. He showed them to the door. "Remember," he said, laying a forefinger over his lips, "not a word to anybody. I must investigate it first."

"Yes, Father."

". . . and the bishop must be informed."

"Yes, Father."

"It would make him very unhappy if there was a scandal."

"Yes, Father," they answered, but an ominous evasiveness clouded their dark eyes, and the priest realized his warning was too late. His eyes followed the sidewalk to the car waiting at the curb and came to rest on Carmen's brother. They had certainly told him; he would tell others. Father Anselmo closed the door behind them and shuddered, hoping only that the situation would remain in his control.

He returned to his breviary, but his mind wandered over the Latin phrases until he closed the book altogether, rationalizing that such tattered prayers were more offensive to God than none at all. He walked to the door of the sanctuary and stared at the altar, draped with its shabby linen cloth. The nuns had tried to disguise the worn spots by darning them in the form of so many embroidered crosses, but the patches showed for what they were. Above the tabernacle the Savior's body on the old crucifix hung precariously by one nail and a strand of twisted wire. The paten lay tarnished on the frayed purple cover. The cheap glass cruets were badly chipped—injuries at the hands of clumsy acolytes—and

44

on Sundays the altar rail swayed unsteadily beneath the weight of the communicants' clasped hands.

"*Introibo ad altare Dei,*" he murmured as he crossed the threshold and went down on one knee. The genuflection was a long one and Father Anselmo bowed his head before the dilapidated cross. It was very easy to be humble at the altar of God. He knelt on the first step and raised his eyes to the crucifix. The paint had long since faded from the corpus. The blood drops issuing from the crown of thorns and the swollen wound in the side were now colorless tears.

Miracles had to occur somewhere, he thought . . . as soon in Landry as at Lourdes or Guadalupe. Suddenly he cried aloud: "Did the Lady come to build me a new church?" His hands flew out, palms upward in supplication. "*Neustra Señora del Molino!*" It was an ejaculation of hope.

As his voice died in the dusty shadows he looked over his shoulder to see if he were alone. Pale light filtered through the rose window at the back and spilled into the choir loft. In the blackness below, votive candles flickered like burning rosebuds at the sandled feet of St. Theresa and St. Martin. The sagging door at the side entrance rattled dryly in its frame, an insistent tattoo.

He rose, embarrassed by his outburst, genuflected hastily as he crossed in front of the tabernacle, and slipped through the gate in the communion rail.

He tried to convince himself the fleeting hope was ridiculous. The story of the vision was certainly untrue, as the bishop would be swift to declare, putting an end to the matter. There would be no new church. Father Anselmo sighed unhappily.

He leaned his broad shoulder into the rattling door and shoved it back into the frame, straining with the futility of

45

the act; in another moment the wind would dislodge it once again. No new church, not even sturdier hinges.

His fingers dipped automatically into the holy water font. Dry!

He crossed to the sacristy, returning with a glass of water, and filled the font. Then he dipped his hand in and made the sign of the cross. As he genuflected for the last time he murmured in the direction of the altar, "I'm doing this because I don't want to bother him . . . at least until I am sure. After all, His Excellency is a busy man. . . ."

Roseanne Woodley blocked the drawers of her chiffonier with her outstretched arms. "You just keep your hands off them, Possom!"

Possom tried to approach but was driven off by her flashing eyes. "Honey, I'll get them back for you, I swear to God. But right now I got to use them for a while."

"You're not touching my diamonds, Possom. I wrangled long and hard to get them and now they're mine and mine alone. I won't see you throw them away in some hock shop. I lost my share of the ranch because of you. Now you want me to lose the only other things that got passed on to me!"

"I don't want you to lose anything, honey," Possom whispered ominously, "but if we don't scare up some money quick we're going to lose our fannies, and I mean yours as well as mine."

Roseanne's eyes grew wide, but she stubbornly refused to move. Her voice dropped to a low murmur. "How bad is it, Possom?"

"Bad enough to break me from here to kingdom come."

Roseanne stared past him in thought. "Mama's diamonds aren't worth ten cents. They're all cut wrong, full of little black spots. Why, some of the gold has even turned."

46

Possom slumped down on the bed. "I got to take your car back."

"Like hell you will! I'm not giving up that car after everybody in town has seen me in it."

"But I ain't got a penny to pay for it!"

She left her defensive position in front of the chiffonier and took up pacing the floor. "I guess things are up to me again. I swan, it's a situation I ought to be used to."

She stopped her pacing and pointed a finger at him. "Where would you be without me, Possom?"

He stared miserably at the pattern in the rug and rubbed his hands together. "Oh, Roseanne honey . . ."

"Shaddup, Possom, I'm thinking."

She resumed her rapid circuit of the room, filling the air with a trail of cigarette smoke. Finally she stopped and reached for the phone.

Possom looked up expectantly. "Have you come up with something?"

She answered, talking mostly to herself. "It burns me up to think of us grubbing around for a few pennies when Witt Tyler's sitting out there with all the money in the world."

"You mean you're calling Witt?"

"Do I look like I've gone crazy? I'm calling Seyton. Maybe he knows a way I can get my hands on a little of that fortune without waiting for the old bastard to die."

CHAPTER FIVE

At eight o'clock the next morning the first jammed carload of pilgrims rolled up the Orvilles' caliche road to visit the site of the miraculous vision. By ten o'clock, four or five more cars had followed, their occupants trooping around the barnyard ogling the weathered windmill, oblivious to Mrs. Orville's peevish scrutiny from behind her kitchen curtains. Then, at eleven o'clock, Mrs. Orville hastily dispatched the eldest Sanchez boy to fetch Mr. Orville from the fields.

There had been an accident: when Mr. Orville trudged across the barnyard he found his wife standing over the squashed remains of a chicken lying beside a car. Feathers and dark blood speckled the rusty fender. The driver, a middle-aged, overalled Mexican, fussed nervously with the frayed brim of his straw hat, pumping his shoulders up and down in a helpless shrug.

"I seen it all from the window, E.B.," Mrs. Orville announced, indicating the car, the dead chicken, and the driver with an accusing, all-encompassing sweep of her arm. "He wasn't paying no attention to where he was heading and ran smack into that chicken."

Mr. Orville sucked at his teeth and scratched the back

48

of his leathery neck as he examined the remains of the dead hen. "Lookit that!" he said at last. "She had an egg in her."

"That don't surprise me one tiny bit," responded his wife bitterly. "Can't you see that's ol' Lulu? Best layer I ever had."

"Durn shame."

"More'n a shame, I'm telling you. I counted on them eggs."

The man who killed the chicken followed this conversation between the Orvilles until they paused for breath; then he spoke up timidly: "The little thing ran from that bush over there. I never even saw it until . . ."

He closed his mouth and squirmed under the Orvilles' hostile stare. They resumed their dialogue, an odd give and take as if their parts were rehearsed.

"Poor ol' Lulu."

"Makes me so sad I wanna cry."

"You're not gonna find another like her, I'm here to tell you."

"Whatcha think we oughtta do, E.B.?"

The driver's eyes had been shifting back and forth between the couple and settled on Mr. Orville for his answer.

"Well, no amount of grieving or complaining is gonna bring ol' Lulu back to life. The least this fella here can do is pay us for the loss."

They fixed their gaze on him. His hand flew automatically to his empty pockets.

"I don't think a dollar is too steep, do you, *amigo?*" Mr. Orville asked.

"I . . . I don't have no dollar, sir."

Mr. Orville scrutinized the car. "You mean to say that among the whole passel in there you can't scrape together one buck?"

The passengers—his wife, his children, his in-laws—peered apprehensively from the open windows.

Mr. Orville directed his next remark to his wife, but loudly enough to be overheard: "You know, I could have the whole kit'n caboodle arrested for trespassing on private land."

The driver's eyes widened. "The gate was open, sir. . . ."

An excited gabble arose in the car, interrupting him. Then a nervous *"pssst."*

The driver slunk away and stuck his head in the window. After a frantic whispered consultation he shuffled back to the Orvilles holding something in his hand. Mr. Orville stepped back cautiously.

"Here is the dollar, sir," the driver said, opening his fingers to a collection of coins in his palm.

Mr. Orville stared at him a moment in silence before extending his hand for the money. The coins felt warm as they dropped into his palm. He slipped them into his pocket one by one, counting them by touch.

Another *"pssst"* from the car prodded the driver to continue: "Sir, my wife she want to know if we can still visit the shrine."

"He means the windmill, E.B.," Mrs. Orville explained.

"Sure," Mr. Orville said, showing his palms magnanimously. "You can look at it till you're blue in the face, but I'm warning you there ain't nothing to see excepting a dirty water stain."

The driver nodded his head politely, but the fishy look in his eyes hinted he knew something Mr. Orville didn't.

As the car bounced away over potholes toward the windmill, Mr. Orville jingled the coins in the pocket of his jeans.

"Poor ol' Lulu," Mrs. Orville said, picking up where she left off.

50

"Bull corn!" Mr. Orville replied. "I'll take a quick greenback any day of the week."

After a second's shocked silence Mrs. Orville giggled conspiratorially. "Maybe I can shoo another chicken under the wheels of the next car that comes along."

"Then you better get a move on." He gave his head a jerk toward the gate. She looked up in time to see a car rattle over the cattle guard.

"Lordie, what do you suppose gets into people to set 'em to driving all the way out here just to look at an old windmill?" she asked.

"I don't know, but lookit there! Yonder comes one more fool turning off the highway."

"We oughtta close that gate, E.B., and put up a sign saying 'keep out.' "

"Hmmm," Mr. Orville replied. He scratched the back of his neck and squinted at the highway, where still another visitor was slowing for the turnoff. "I just come up with a better idea. . . ."

When Hector Sanchez came home to his shack for lunch he found no less than a dozen cars huddled in the barnyard. A good-sized crowd milled around the windmill's base, chattering brightly, in a festive spirit.

He sought out his wife and grabbed her roughly by the arm. "You foolish woman! Look at those cars and all the people. Mr. Orville is going to fire me."

"No!" Carmen ducked her head, fearing a blow. "He is happy they're here. Come, look and see!"

She dragged him to the open gate, where one of her sons perched on a fence post cradling a cigar box in his lap. At his feet a huge, crudely lettered sign proclaimed in English and Spanish:

172233

Athens Regional Library
Athens, Georgia

MIRACLE! SEE THE LADY OF THE WINDMILL—
50¢ PER CAR!

"Mama!" the boy cried, flipping open the lid. "There is already fourteen dollars!"

"See!" Carmen said triumphantly. "Mr. Orville put up the sign himself. He says everyone can come as long as they pay."

A car bounded up the caliche road with another following immediately in its trail of dust.

Hector watched in disgust as his son snatched the money and waved the car through. "God will punish you," he warned his wife, wrenching himself free of her grip. She crossed herself briskly to exorcise the curse.

The second car pulled up, paid, and moved through the gate.

In the yard, Noelia was repeating the story for the newcomers. ". . . And the Lady said she would give health and happiness to people who pray here." As she paused to wipe away a film of moisture dampening her upper lip, the crowd took the opportunity to press forward. Rosaries rattled between their fingers as they waited for her to continue. They had been hanging on every word.

But Noelia kept the next part to herself, the Lady's pledge that her own prayer would be fulfilled. Once again, before picking up the story, she searched for the promised *Señor* among the eager faces surrounding her. They stared back, hungry for more. Wives with their husbands, clinging children, *abuelas* half hidden in black mantillas with wilting wild flower bouquets for the shrine, a toothless old man hobbling arthritically on a knurled cane. But no sign of *el Señor*, not yet.

She sucked in a sharp breath, confident but impatient, and went on with her recital: ". . . and then there was so much light, *aiii,* that I had to close my eyes. When I opened them again the Lady was gone."

"*Aiii . . .*" echoed the crowd in soft sympathy, downcast

52

Athens Regional Library
Athens, Georgia

that there was no more to hear. The old man rattled his cane feebly, lisping, *"Qué lástima . . . qué lástima!"*

Noelia let them fret for another moment before springing her surprise, the *pelón* they were dying for. "But she left behind her image. *There!"* She pointed a finger at the windmill. "There! In the wood. Can you see it?"

Her audience wheeled about, sweeping the water-stained strut with their eyes, eager to be the first to spot the Lady's miraculous imprint.

"Aiiii!" A gray-haired *abuela* sank to her knees with a joyful shudder, her hand flying about her face in a score of busy crosses. "I see, I see!"

Noelia was suddenly forgotten. The others left her, swarming around the windmill, squinting up at its braces, searching the wood grain for the Virgin's image. One after another cried out, crossed himself, and dropped to his knees. The old man extended a trembling hand, catching in the air a winking drop of water that spilled from the overflow pipe on the adjacent tank.

Mr. Orville watched from the kitchen window as the man dabbed the water against his arthritic joints. "If that old hombre turns up frisky as a colt, I'm gonna take a swim in that tank!"

Mrs. Orville joined her husband at the window. "Lordie, E.B., there must be fifteen or twenty cars piled up out there. You better get yourself over to the gate and empty the cigar box before that Sanchez kid takes a notion to line his pockets."

"Hmmm," Mr. Orville said, straightening up. "I expect you're right."

Witt heard about the vision the next morning from E. B. Orville himself. He had driven into Landry as far as the Farmers' Exchange to buy a box of flea powder for Minnie, who had kept him awake a good part of the night scratching with noisy thumps at her scruffy neck in the bushes beneath his bedroom window.

As he waited for his change, E. B. Orville entered the store and ordered a coil of barbed wire. "I gotta build me a fence," he informed Witt, standing next to him at the counter. "The wife's vegetable garden is getting trampled to bits."

"Is that a fact?" Witt replied. He hadn't the vaguest notion what the man was talking about.

"Yep, stamped to pieces by all them crazy people traipsing out to see my windmill," Mr. Orville added as if that were an explanation.

Witt waited. He could tell by Orville's arched eyebrows and puckered lips that he was going to get the rest of the story.

Orville took a deep breath and continued: "Yessiree, ever since word got out that that oldest Mexican girl that lives on my place saw some kind of Catholic vision, my barnyard's looked like the Zamora County Fair, people all over the place, praying, singing, carrying on like nothing I ever seen. Even was a reporter from the newspaper out there first thing this morning, talking to the girl and snapping pictures like she was some beauty queen. Now, ain't that the limit? He told me it was gonna be on the front page for sure."

Witt took his change from the clerk and touched his brim in farewell to Orville.

"You really oughtta come on out, I'm telling ya," Orville said, reluctant to let a prospective customer slip through his hands. "Everybody's saying there's gonna be a miracle going on, and who can tell . . . maybe they know something I don't."

54

"Well now," said Witt, "I wouldn't mind seeing a miracle, but I got an itchy dog to take care of first."

"Be seeing you," Orville called hopefully.

"Maybe," answered Witt. He stumped down the wooden steps and climbed into his pickup.

Minnie's eyes glazed with relief as Witt dusted the flea powder into her thick gray coat. He could see the tiny black specks leaping from her fur to the ground. The telephone was ringing in the house, but he took time to shake a cloud of powder into each of his boots before climbing the steps to answer it.

It was Katie on the other end: "You're such an old hermit I don't suppose you've heard the news, but the whole town's talking about some kind of miracle. . . ."

"I'm one step ahead of you, Katie. I got it straight from the horse's mouth."

"My, my, how word spreads. Anyway, I'm calling because I'd like to go out and see it."

"Sounds like you're fishing for a ride."

"I don't want to go alone."

The line of cars backed up for over a mile along the highway. It took Witt's pickup a good half hour to reach the gate.

"Look at that!" he exclaimed as the Sanchez boy jumped up on the running board and pointed to the sign. "Seems old man Orville has gone into the miracle business in earnest."

His half-dollar disappeared into the cigar box.

"Good Lord, Witt!" Katie cried. "It looks like an automobile junkyard. I didn't know there were this many cars in all of Landry!"

They parked in a clearing on the edge of a field and made

their way through a maze of bumpers and fenders and steaming radiators into the periphery of the swarming crowd.

"Orville was right, it's a goddamned carnival," Witt muttered. He took Katie by the arm and squeezed forward into the throng. "Get a load of that windmill!"

Big bright clusters of artificial flowers and trailing crepe paper garlands festooned the four legs like ornaments on a Christmas tree. For a nickel, small boys were swinging hand over hand up the cross braces to tack holy cards, religious medals, rosaries, and snapshots of the sick and dead to the few remaining bare spots on the framework's upper reaches.

Alongside, another group of boys clung like monkeys to the water tank, doling out water in paper cups which passed from lip to lip with a reverence due communion wine.

Since early morning, wave after wave of rumors had swept the crowd, stampeding them first this direction, then that: a crippled man stood up and walked! a blind child opened its eyes and saw! a one-armed man suddenly sprouted his missing limb! Almost immediately Witt found himself penned in by an excited mob who, having spotted his eye patch, were intent on witnessing the miraculous restoration of his eye.

"Leave me be! Go find yourselves another miracle!" He crushed his hat brim close over his forehead, angry and embarrassed. "Come on, Katie, I've had enough. Let's clear out of here."

"Wait, Witt! Not yet." She laid her hand imploringly on his arm. "Not just yet, please." Her cheeks were flushed with a strange fire. She plunged ahead deeper into the crowd, keeping her unblinking eyes on the spinning windmill. Witt shook off his disappointed following and pushed after her.

A quarter of a mile back in the long unmoving line on the highway, Father Anselmo sat steaming in his stalled car. Nervous perspiration constricted his Roman collar into a choking noose until his eyes bulged from their sockets. He could think of nothing but the bishop's angry outrage sure to come when news of the vision madness reached him. How was he going to answer the inevitable interrogation: *What steps did you take to prevent this scandal to Holy Mother Church?*

The damp noose tightened and Father Anselmo hung his head through the window gasping for air. He heard his earnest prayers for a promotion, a better posting, or at least sufficient funds to build a new church fading like hollow echoes along with his reputation.

Over the car tops and the pilgrims' bobbing heads the gaily decorated windmill mocked him like an insolent, painted woman. He could stand it no longer. Crying, "Sacrilege!" he yanked his car onto the shoulder of the road, flew from the door, and scrambled through the barbed wire.

The sight of the black-suited priest kicking up dust over the field's deep furrows alarmed those still waiting on the highway. They tensed, hearts fluttering, convinced the rumored miracle was taking place without them. All along the road doors swung open. A shrieking flood of people surged over the fence and streamed across the plowed land in hot pursuit of the priest.

Father Anselmo charged into the barnyard. He elbowed his way through the packed mob, exhorting them: "Go home! I order it! This is a trick of the devil!" But the noisy excitement swallowed up his voice and he was lost in their midst.

Dressed only in her thin cotton slip, Noelia huddled in the safety of her bed, still trembling with fright at her narrow escape. She had been halfway through her story when someone in the crush around her suddenly screamed, *"Santa Noelia!"* The crowd reacted in a frenzy of religious fervor. Fingers clawed the air to get a touch of their new saint. They snatched for her hair, her bracelet, her earrings, any souvenir. In another instant they fell upon her, shredding the dress from her

57

back. Even as Carmen seized her about the waist and strong-armed a path to their shack, the snarling relic hunters hurled themselves after her, tugging at her sandals until the straps burst their threads and the shoes fell from her feet.

Now, with Carmen mumbling the prayers of the rosary beside her, she sat half kneeling on the hard mattress, eyes wet with tears but too stunned and bewildered to cry.

Across the way, Mrs. Orville had also barricaded herself in, opening the door only when Mr. Orville made his half-hourly appearance with another bagful of money. This she snatched from his excited hands and emptied with a clatter into a rapidly filling washtub. Hours before, she had stopped counting the take. The sum had grown so large her agitated mind no longer trusted her figuring.

On his latest trip to the house with another bulging bundle, Mrs. Orville dragged her husband inside the door and pleaded: "That's enough, E.B.! Make them go home!"

Mr. Orville was so astonished by his wife's suggestion that for a moment he couldn't speak. Finally he gulped several times and said, "Are you crazy? I never seen so much money in all my life!"

Mrs. Orville's face was stiff and white. She backed away, refusing the bag he shoved at her. "I think it's a sin, E.B.!"

"Bull corn!" he shouted. "If these people want to get rid of their money, the Lord won't mind me obliging them. Besides, don't tell me you've gone and fell for that girl's crazy story."

Mrs. Orville shook her head and let herself be handed the money.

"That's better," he said as the coins jingled from the bag into the tub. "Now, listen to me and hear what I want you to do. Rummage through the house and scare up every sody bottle you can lay your hands on. Then get up in the attic and fetch down my old bottle capper. These people are drinking up our water like they was expecting a drought. We might as well make a few pennies out of that too."

"E.B.!" she cried. Her mouth fell open.

"Don't E.B. me!" he ordered, girding himself to slip back out the door. "Just get to hunting for them bottles."

In her effort to maneuver closer to the windmill, Katie had led Witt deeper into the crowd until they found themselves shoved up against the flaking boards of Hector Sanchez's shack. There Katie paused and sought out the indistinct stain that marked the focus of veneration. As she gazed up at the spinning windmill, lost in thought, Witt heard a rustling sound behind him and turned to find himself staring directly into Noelia's startled face. Six inches of space and a tattered window screen separated them.

He smiled at her.

For a moment Noelia made no response. Then her eyelids lowered, the thick lashes fluttering, flickering, before lifting again above wet brown eyes. Suddenly her mouth curved at the corners showing her even white teeth in an answering smile, for she had noticed in Witt's blue-white iris a significant, portentous, unmistakable pinpoint of light.

CHAPTER SIX

"Hello," Witt said.

"Hello, *Señor,*" Noelia replied.

His eye twinkled . . . unnecessarily: she had not missed the sign. With coquet slowness that managed to look demure she gathered the rumpled sheet around her throat. Her thick black hair slithered over the curve of her neck and coiled into a glistening knot in her lap. She lifted her hand to brush it out of her eyes, revealing a glimpse of bare brown arm creased white where the slip cut across her shoulder.

"*Cómo se llama usted?*" he asked.

"Noelia," the girl answered. She smiled again.

"*Me llamo* Witt," he said.

"*Encantada,*" Noelia replied. She inclined her head forward, ever so slightly—but to Witt the gesture was a courtly, gracious curtsy. He swept his hat from his head and bowed, as well as he could with the crush of the crowd against him. Then straightening he leaned close to the screen and asked: "Are you the one who saw the Lady?"

She nodded eagerly, drawn into the pale blue eye. "What did she look like?"

Her face brushed the screen, nodding like a heavy bloom. "Oh! so pretty, so beautiful, more than I can say."

Her dark hair so close to him teased his nostrils with a sensual, shadowy fragrance, a warm caressing perfume of night.

Before he could speak again a sharp voice flew out of the shadow behind her: *"Noelia!"*

"It's my mother." She drew away from the screen, showing again the satiny curve of a smooth brown shoulder above the edge of the sheet.

Witt winked his one eye slowly—total darkness. When he raised the lid again he found she was gone.

"Noelia," he whispered, almost to himself, half in hope his gentle calling would draw her again to the screen. But the window remained empty, leaving him alone with the memory of her face nodding toward him close enough to be stroked by his fingertips. His throat tightened. A chill stiffened the short hair on his neck.

Katie was squeezing his hand. She pulled him out of the spell. She had grown restless again, tight-faced and strained.

"I want to go closer," she said.

He moved mechanically, letting himself be led through the crowd until they stood directly beside the windmill. Flowers and sinuous streamers fluttered lazily in the braces above their heads. She let go of him and lowered her eyes, trying to formulate a prayer. She would have done anything, lighted candles, burned incense, slaughtered a lamb, perched on a flagpole, donned a hair shirt, anything, if she had thought it would work. "Let me hear that Wally is alive," she begged silently. "If you really can do miracles, this one should be worthwhile. It's a life I'm asking for. Make him be alive. Send him home to me, please. I believe in you! If that's what you want, I really believe in you! I believe I believe I believe. . . ."

Witt watched her moving lips, suspecting what was going

on in her mind. He had to speak her name several times before she looked up and focused on him.

He put his arm gently around her waist. He spoke softly in her ear. "Let's go, Katie. I think it's time we left."

That night Minnie, flea-free at last, slept soundly beneath the bedroom window, leaving Witt undisturbed to dream.

It was a straightforward dream, innocent of symbols that would have escaped him anyway. Noelia came to him from across a sweeping field of tall green grass, cutting a swath with flying strides through the slender, supple blades that whipped and bowed beneath the warm blowing wind. The grass bent before her legs, thrashed wildly against the billowing umbrella of her skirt, and snapped back into a flashing wake behind her, glistening with green fire in the hard shadowless sunlight of high noon.

It seemed to take forever for her to cross the meadow. He strained toward her, thrusting out his impatient arms in welcome. When she had covered about half the distance between them, Witt saw that she was breathing hard. Her long hair rose and fell with every labored step, fanning out shiny and black like the mane of a frolicking colt.

"Faster, Noelia, hurry, hurry! Can't you see I haven't much time!" he shouted. "I'm getting old. There's no holding it back. Hurry, hurry!"

She was close . . . very close. He could see her swinging hair, her nostrils flaring with every quick breath. He could hear her puffing, could feel her hot breath exploding from her pretty lips striking against his face.

All at once she was there. They touched! She collapsed into his arms. He held her close, kissed her forehead, then her eyes. He buried his face in the warm midnight perfume of her

62

hair. When her breathing calmed and her heart ceased to pound so thunderously against his chest they turned around and began walking hand in hand from the meadow.

Suddenly she stiffened against him. She pulled him to a halt. On the edge of the field near a row of dark trees stood Roseanne, flanked by Seyton and Floyd. Their shouts were lost in the noisy pockets of wind, but Witt understood the threats of their clenched fists and contorted faces. He looked at them for a moment as if amused by the display. Then slowly and deliberately he raised his fist to his puckered lips, extending all fingers except for the first, which made an O with the thumb. From behind this improvised megaphone he let fly a wet, buzzing raspberry.

His own delighted laughter woke him. He rolled over and howled into his pillow. It was morning. In the distance the oil pumps were working quietly. He lay in bed listening to their constant rhythm, as regular as the gentle breathing of a sleeping person. He closed his eye and pretended the sound of the nearest was Noelia: she was lying beside him. The others were their children, soft baby snores from all the other rooms of the house. . . .

Roseanne sent up her call for help and her brothers responded, but reluctantly, unhappy to be dragged into a crisis that called for money.

Possom, looking natty despite disaster, though properly abashed, let them in as they arrived one by one. First Seyton, the lawyer, shaking his round pink face and tutting like a feisty schoolmaster. Then the Reverend Floyd Tyler, younger but balder, swallowing his anger behind tight jaws. Finally Emmett, the eldest, who had slipped almost completely into a cloud of senility. He arrived late, having forgotten the meeting.

63

He alone showed up with a vague but genuine smile for Possom, who sat down beside him across from the sulfurous scowls of the other two.

Roseanne was avoiding her husband completely. It strained her soul to remain in the same room with him.

Seyton started off. "I been mulling over what you said on the phone, Roseanne, and it sure looks like Possom's landed himself in a pretty fix."

Emmett smiled again at Possom as if he had just been complimented. Possom squirmed.

"Well now, that's what I call a brilliant observation," Roseanne snapped. "Your turn, Floyd. I guess you're going to say you've been praying for us!"

"Simmer down," Seyton clucked. "We're not here to fuss with each other. We've come to save Possom's hide."

"Lord knows how," Floyd muttered.

Roseanne lit a cigarette and blew smoke halfway across the room. "I've set my sights on Witt. He's damn near the richest man in the world and never spends a penny. If we could get our hands on . . ."

Floyd's eyes rolled back in his head.

Seyton broke into a chuckle, bubbling up from his round belly. "Heaven help us, Roseanne! Have you been sitting out in the sun too long? You'd have better luck knocking on the door at Fort Knox."

Roseanne bit her lip, angry at the jibe.

"Let's leave Witt out of this from the start," Floyd said. "We've had nothing to do with him for forty years, it wouldn't be Christian to go badgering him for money now."

"You're right, Floyd," Seyton said, then to Roseanne: "Floyd's right. The less we have to do with Witt the better. I don't even like to recall he's part of the family. He's the only one of us Tylers that never amounted to a hill of beans."

"Some hill!" Roseanne said.

"I ain't talking about money. He didn't do nothing to earn it. I'm talking about reputation. Well, he's old and slowed down now. I don't reckon we'll be hearing much more out of him. The situation suits me just fine. As long as he don't do nothing to worry me or scandal the family name I don't figure on bothering him."

"Shoot," Roseanne said, snapping an ash into the empty fireplace. "I don't have any fancy qualms about that. If I could get to it I'd sooner use his money than any of yours."

Seyton and Floyd looked as if they had been strangled. "Our money! Roseanne, honey, neither one of us has a red cent to spare. You got any idea what my expenses are?"

"Everybody knows about us preachers, one step up from a pauper!" Floyd feigned a shudder.

A long raspy snore rocked the room.

"Wake Emmett up. He's gone to sleep again."

Emmett had slumped forward, breathing noisily through his gaping mouth. Possom extended his leg and gave Emmett's shoe a nudge. Emmett snorted, smacked his lips, and opened his eyes. He didn't know where he was, but seeing the family gathered together, asked brightly: "Is it Christmas?"

"Pay attention, Emmett," Roseanne said, "or we'll put you away."

Emmett smiled around the room, thinking Roseanne had made a joke. He shrank back from the reproving faces that greeted him, yawned, and slipped away again.

"What the hell, let him sleep," Possom said. To his surprise no one objected. He looked up and saw all eyes on Emmett.

"Hush!" Roseanne ordered, although no one but Emmett was making a sound, snoring fitfully. It was just her way of saying she was about to speak. "Emmett's got the ranch and a couple of wells. Wouldn't that make pretty hefty collateral at any bank?"

"What are you getting at, Roseanne?"

She marched across the room, whipped around and faced them with flashing eyes. "Look, if we can get Emmett over to some bank in Corpus we could nail down a loan on the strength of his property. It's easy as pie. Then Possom delivers the pipe, pays the loan back, and Emmett's no worse for the wear."

The three men looked at Emmett. He had crumpled sideways on the couch, nestled happily into the cushions.

"Don't hardly seem right. Poor old thing won't know what he's doing."

Roseanne waved Seyton away. "That makes it even better. It won't worry him none."

Floyd held up his finger. "What about Willy-boy?"

This stopped Roseanne. She stood in the middle of the floor shredding an empty cigarette package with her bright red fingernails while she thought of how to cope with Emmett's son.

Seyton came to the rescue, eager to help now that Roseanne was looking to Emmett for the money instead of to him. "Willy-boy ain't too bright. Besides, he's all the time buried out there on the ranch. He don't have to know."

"And how do you propose to keep Emmett from telling?"

"Shoot! He talks so much gibberish anyway that nobody half listens. Willy-boy'll just think his daddy dreamed the whole thing up."

Floyd glanced at Seyton. As if on signal they rose, eager to be gone before Roseanne changed her mind.

"I'll check around," Seyton said, reaching for his hat and sidling toward the door. "I'll find us a bank we can count on being friendly."

66

Floyd followed on his heels.

When the door closed behind them Roseanne turned to Possom, her eyes glittering through narrow slits. "You ought to thank your lucky stars I got smart brothers like that."

Possom shuddered. "I'm just glad they're on my side."

She glared at him, suspicious of his tone. Emmett's snores continued. "Let him sleep here tonight," she said, snapping off the outside light. "Too risky to make him drive home. I don't want our investment falling asleep behind the wheel. And get a blanket to throw over him so he won't catch pneumonia and die."

Father Anselmo's fingers trembled as he struck a match and held it to the wick of a votive candle at St. Theresa's feet. The yellow flame sputtered in the crimson cup. A trace of pale smoke writhed upward into the plaster folds of the saint's garments. He bowed his head, burying his tortured brow in his hands, and tried to pray.

He had known the bishop would be angry, anticipated a reprimand, expected to be called upon to explain his delay in informing his superior of the alleged vision. But he had been totally unprepared for the vehemence of the bishop's language.

"Shameful scandal," the episcopal letter had admonished beneath the diocesan seal. Even worse, it accused him of sinful negligence. It ordered an immediate halt to the pagan worship and demanded his appearance before His Excellency himself.

Father Anselmo raised his troubled eyes to the statue's placid face. "Help me, please!" he pleaded.

He was only vaguely aware of the telephone's prolonged ringing in his office.

At the other end, waiting impatiently for the priest to answer, was Mr. Orville. Though Father Anselmo would

67

attribute the call to St. Theresa's direct intervention forever after, Mr. Orville's motivation sprang from a more mundane source. As he stood at the kitchen window with the ringing phone to his ear, he surveyed with mounting horror the shambles before him.

The crowd outside was thicker than ever, overflowing into the distant fields beyond the fences, which, along with every last chicken, had been trampled underfoot. No trace remained of the concrete watering trough, or of the two young cedars he had planted the year before. That morning the main gate had gone, ripped down by an angry mob when they found it padlocked and marked with a sign prohibiting entry. The groaning windmill itself was threatening collapse beneath the fervor of relic seekers whittling away splinters from the four legs.

Coins and crumpled dollar bills filled the zinc tub to capacity. Mrs. Orville's fingers ached from hours of operating the bottle cap machine. But they had both decided, appalled by the growing havoc and frightened for their own safety, that they had had enough of the miracle business.

Mr. Orville was calling to beg Father Anselmo to do something to keep his flock away. But his wife, hovering nervously beside him, was pleading in a tiny quivering voice: "The police, E.B., the police! You should be calling the police!"

CHAPTER SEVEN

Like thunder from a heat-born summer storm the rumor broke across the county: Father Anselmo had orders to close down the shrine!

At daybreak the next day, pilgrim-packed cars started rolling out of town forming a stretched-out, crawling caravan on the highway to the farm. They jammed up and ground to a bumper-to-bumper halt outside the demolished gate. Facing them, forbidding them to enter, was a jittery line of gray-shirted policemen summoned from Landry at Mrs. Orville's insistence. The lawmen toted rifles and squinted at the growing throng in the rising sun's hard glare. The dew still twinkled on the trampled grass. To keep their boots dry the policemen took to standing on the flattened posts that once formed Mr. Orville's fence. They kept their eyes on the crowd.

People climbed out of their cars but held back along the road's white shoulder, glum-faced, angry, and apprehensive. The rifles kept them from overrunning the police line as they once overran the gate. Instead, they milled about, speaking softly like funeral-goers, and cast longing glances at the forlorn windmill rising out of the rubble.

As the morning grew older and the crowd grew larger, the policemen shifted uneasily from one boot to the other, hiking their rifles higher on their shoulders, always watching . . . watching with sharp flicking movements of their wary eyes.

Inside their kitchen, the Orvilles relieved their nervous pacing by leaning against the drainboard and gulping black coffee from their second pot. They cocked impatient ears for Father Anselmo's arrival.

Across the farmyard Noelia lay suffering in her bed. She knew what was going to happen. Hector had been called to the Orvilles' house late the night before. When he returned he broke the news to her. The hours dragged through the long night. She had slept very little, dropping off in the middle of a prayer to reawaken with a start, believing she once again heard the tinkling shower of heavenly bells. But each time, as her heart's noisy racket receded from her ears, she strained against the open window and heard nothing but the mocking wind brushing through the trees and the nearby dreamless breathing of her family.

Now they too were awake and stirring. They kept to themselves, avoiding her corner of the room as if she had been quarantined. From time to time as they splashed their faces with water and pulled on their clothes, they sneaked furtive looks at her supine figure as if, at any moment, they were likely to find themselves gazing upon a corpse.

Father Anselmo approached, zigzagging a path through the maze of automobiles. The lawmen quickly waved him past. He was sweating profusely, too overwrought to hear the crowd's greeting, an agonized moaning sigh. Their hearts ached. The rumor was true! In the seat behind him he carried two pails of black paint and wide brushes.

As he drew near to the house, the Orvilles' faces, two pale moons, floated to the window like wan lamps.

Witt had heard the rumor along with everyone else. After

Minnie roused him with halfhearted barking at what her near-sighted eyes identified as a scampering mouse but which was really a fuzzy gray woolie blown along by the wind, he dressed, set his hat squarely on his head, and stamped down the steps.

The door of the sagging shed out back creaked as he strained to wrest it open. Red dust flaked from the rusty hinges. At last the door gave, not at the frozen latch but down the rotting middle planks, leaving him holding half the door. He heaved it to the side out of the way and kicked the other side open. Inside, under an enormous tarpaulin shroud, was his Rolls-Royce. He pulled the canvas from the car and shoved it with his boot against the wall. Even in the shed's dim light the car gleamed like new.

"Come on, Minnie," he said. He had to coax her with little clucks into the front seat. He fished the key from his pocket and slipped it into the ignition lock. He hoped there was gas; he had no idea—it was ages since he had driven the thing. There was always the pickup in case he had to siphon. Today especially he wanted to drive the big car.

He turned the key. The gas gauge jumped. He was delighted. The engine caught immediately. He ran his hand over Minnie's old head and waited for the engine to warm up. Then he released the brake and glided backward, almost silently, out of the shed.

As he neared the Orvilles' farm, the police, wary of the crowd and unprepared for the sight of the one-eyed man and his dog sharing the front seat of the massive car, stepped aside, letting him motor unmolested across the cattle guard. He pulled up beside a splintered cedar stump. The place looked like a battlefield. He observed the Orvilles and Father Anselmo shouldering rakes, marching in single file across the yard to the base of the venerated windmill.

71

Without a word to one another they raised their tools into the air and swept them over the windmill, scraping down the paper flowers, the faded curling photographs, the sad wilted ribbons, and—though it troubled Father Anselmo's soul—the rosaries, tarnished medals, and dew-limp holy cards.

The Sanchezes, with the exception of Noelia, appeared at their back door—emerging one after the other like successive boxes of a Chinese puzzle. They watched with stolid, unfathomable expressions as the regalia fell in sorry tatters around the wooden legs.

When they had swept the timbers clean as far as they could reach, Mr. Orville climbed the rough ladder and raked the rest of the fluttering objects from the higher struts. They drifted to the ground in swirling somersaults, tracing weary coils through the air like autumn leaves joining the growing pile of trash.

Along the road the crowd had fallen into shocked silence. The policemen, still showing their weapons, allowed their eyes quick glances at the activity in the barnyard. When Mr. Orville finished stripping the windmill bare of the remaining holy cards he cast away the rake and descended the ladder almost to the bottom. With his feet on the lowest rung, hanging on with one hand, he waited for Father Anselmo and Mrs. Orville to pry the lids from the pails. They stirred the black paint with slats of wood gathered from the debris around them. Father Anselmo stood up and passed a pail and a brush to Mr. Orville, who made his way carefully back up the ladder until he was just below the languidly turning blades of the windmill.

He paused, as if listening for someone unseen to tell him where to begin. Then he grasped the brush, sank its bristles deep into the glistening paint, and slapped a wet black swath across the timbers.

A rivulet of paint from the overloaded brush broke away. It oozed quickly along the wood's grain until its ragged trickle streaked across the brownish parabola that had first sent Carmen to her knees. This time Carmen merely closed her eyes and shuddered against Hector, who looked on with grim relief.

But the crowd raised a cry from the road, a mournful wail that reached Mr. Orville. He paused on his perch and stared at them over his shoulder. The nervous policemen tightened up on their rifles. But instantly they instinctively recognized the groan as a thing of sadness and loss, not a warning of danger. They became embarrassed by their weapons and let them slip into positions next to their legs, as if to hide them.

Minnie rested her muzzle on Witt's shoulder. He circled his arm around her neck and scratched her head, watching through the windshield as Father Anselmo took the other brush and set to work on the windmill's base.

As the two areas of fresh paint spread toward the middle, reaching for each other, the Sanchez family left their back door and huddled in a knot beside the overturned water trough. Witt saw Noelia was not with them. His pale eye swung back to the shack and caught a ghostly white movement behind the screen. It hovered in the window for an instant and then vanished abruptly into the shadows. He shrugged Minnie's muzzle off his shoulder. With a sniff of resignation, the dog crept onto the floorboard, settling her head between her paws.

Witt swung open the door and stepped out into the sun. He crossed the rutted, littered yard to the little house.

Even as he leaned close to the screen door, shading the glare with his flattened palm, he had no real idea of what he was going to do. He peered inside. Noelia was on the floor, half sitting, half kneeling beside her bed like a crouched animal. Her face was buried in her hands. The sunlight streamed across the room striking against the long black hair that fanned over her shoulders.

As he opened the door and stepped inside, she dropped her hands and looked up. Tears were streaking her cheeks, making her skin glisten like wet glass.

He dropped to his knees beside her.

Her raised face was drawn with pain. "Señor Witt! I want to die!"

His hands flew out to her but stopped short of her shoulders. He trembled, afraid for the first time in his life to touch a woman. Noelia would not wait. She closed her eyes and threw herself into his arms.

Hoarse ragged sobs tore from her throat. She shook violently as she pressed close to him, crying, "I want to die! I want to die!"

All Witt could do was say, "Shhh . . ." He stroked her hair with his fingers. She seemed to have no weight against him, like a bird perched on his shoulder. He supported her tenderly, repeating softly, "Shhh . . . shhh . . ."

When the trembling subsided he lifted her to her feet. With an arm around her waist he escorted her to the door. She walked with him from the house without the slightest pause, as if her acquiescence had been preordained, decreed by the Lady's promise. They moved slowly, holding on to one another, across the barnyard to the waiting car.

The painters had very nearly reached midpoint, commanding all eyes as the last few feet of bare wood disappeared beneath their brushes. Witt and Noelia slipped into the car, unobserved.

He started the motor. The car made a wide circle, scattering the paper flowers which had blown beneath its wheels. The police line again parted at the gateway. The car slipped past,

74

moving through the crowd as unhampered and unnoticed as a simple breeze.

Forty miles away, in Corpus Christi, Roseanne and Possom climbed out of her Cadillac and joined her brothers on the steps outside the bank Seyton had decided on.

Inside they found the procedure a piece of cake. Possom kept quiet. Seyton had never been so eloquent. Roseanne looked prim. Floyd added dignity. And Emmett stayed awake.

Not even Possom's unsuppressed sigh of relief when the check was carried in managed to upset Roseanne. She was busily thinking: now Possom can transfer that pipe and pay for my Cadillac. She glanced across the room, granting Emmett a set smile much as one mugs at a baby to divert its attention. He smiled back, sitting very erect, maintaining a façade of bright alertness. For a fleeting moment she toyed with the idea of paying him interest but shook the thought out of her head. Emmett was too old and too rich for a few dollars to make any difference. Her eyes narrowed: Now, if it had been Witt, if she had gotten control of his money . . .

"It's too hot a trip for Emmett in Seyton's old unair-conditioned car," Roseanne said, once they were back outside. With the check safely in her handbag she could afford gratitude. She grabbed him by the arm and steered him toward her Cadillac. "Let him ride with me."

As they headed onto the open highway, Possom propped a foot on the dashboard, unbuttoned his coat, thrusting out his chest, and said, "Man alive, I'm glad that's over with! Now I'm back in business."

Roseanne knocked his foot from the dash with a savage slap. "We saved your hide, you sonuvabitch! Now, you deliver that pipe and settle down. In the future I don't want to hear

75

that you've got anything cooking unless you've checked the ingredients with me first."

Possom rubbed his calf where Roseanne had stung him. A scuff mark remained on the dashboard. He hoped she wouldn't notice.

She was busy checking the rearview mirror to see if Emmett had dozed off. "Listen to me good, Possom. You get that money for the pipe so we can settle your debts and pay back this loan. Lordie, if anything goes wrong and that goddamn bank claims his ranch, Willy-boy'll be coming after us with a loaded shotgun. As far as you're concerned I think it might be a good idea to get out of the pipe business altogether."

"But, Roseanne . . ."

"Things aren't operating the way they used to. I'm not about to gallivant around to every bank in South Texas every two weeks begging for a handout."

She knocked a cigarette from a fresh pack with one hand and snapped it between her red lips. Possom struck a match and held it up.

She French-inhaled and blew the smoke away. "I'll think of something that'll keep you out of trouble. In the meantime you're on vacation."

Begrudgingly, Possom nodded obediently. Later, when he was sure she wasn't looking, he rubbed away the scuff mark with the cuff of his coat.

"This is my place," Witt said to Noelia as they drove up to the house. He noticed another bare spot on the roof where a loose shingle had finally rotted through and fallen off. They left the car and started forward, Minnie leading the way toward the porch.

"Careful on those steps," he warned. "Couple of boards missing on the third one up."

Noelia took the hand he offered her and negotiated the steps. Dry weeds pushed up through the hole. As soon as he opened the front door and let her into the living room he wished he had kept her outside.

She made her way to the center of the cavernous room. Warped floorboards shrieked beneath the threadbare carpet. A dismal gray light struggled through dusty panes, cracked and patched with cardboard squares. He saw afresh, as if they belonged to a stranger, the battered furniture, the shapeless couch that sagged on three legs, the lamps with no shades. Her finger trailed a tabletop bearing scars from the heels of his boots.

He watched with a sinking feeling as her eyes dropped from the brown water stains on the ceiling to the floor below, where dripping rain had etched white circles on the hardwood.

"Maybe you'd rather sit out on the porch? It's not so gloomy . . ." His voice trailed off helplessly.

She seemed not to have heard. She had moved to the doorway and was staring wide-eyed down the hall.

"What's the matter?"

She didn't answer . . . not until he joined her and looked down the hallway through the far door to the bathroom at the other end. "Would you mind," she said at last, "if I used that toilet?"

He waited for her on the back porch, feeling ridiculous and old. He was ashamed of his house and of himself. He swore at the foolishness that tricked him to thinking he could turn an old man's dream into reality. He moved to the edge of the porch and made his decision: he would take her back to her family.

He rested his elbows on the railing and swept his eye along the encircling horizon. It was a pencil line of enclosing loneliness, the boundaries of his ranch, of all he owned. And empty. Empty! During the war he fought to keep the old steel oil derricks that sprouted like a crowded forest from the house for as far as he could see. It was something to look at. It was company. But they needed the metal and the towers came down.

Now the house loomed like an eroding island in the desert of glaring caliche dust. Just Witt and his dog. He felt marooned.

The sun beat down relentlessly, making the horizon swim with rising air currents. A quick hot wind whipped up with a dry ugly rattle.

Witt stared in horror. Something was moving through the rippling heat, something dark and final swinging along the horizon's blurry arc. He blinked. It was a figure astride a galloping horse. The figure rose, standing in the stirrups as if searching the distance for something. It could have been anyone, a neighbor or a wrangler after a stray calf. But what Witt saw was Death riding by.

"So that's how it starts," he thought. "He's taking my measure. He's scouting my field, sweeping by for a look before he commits himself." His heart turned cold. He thought he felt an icy finger run across his forehead, marking him. Despite the searing wind, he shivered uncontrollably. He rubbed his face with both hands to obliterate the chilly mark. "No, by God! Not me . . . not yet!"

Turning around, he found Noelia standing silently in the doorway. She held a broom in her hand.

He smiled bitterly. He took the broom from her and leaned it against the outside wall. "You don't have to bother with that." His voice was tired. His face was beaten and weary. "I know the place is a mess."

She stared at him with troubled eyes.

"Come on," he said, avoiding her look. "I'll take you back home. You must be tired."

78

Her face collapsed. *"No!"* she cried. She threw herself against the door he was trying to open. Thoughts flooded through her brain, of the big rooms she had just explored on her way back through the house, of the gas range and the refrigerator, and the indoor bathroom with its footed tub and flush toilet. She shook her head and screamed, "Don't make me go away!"

He quit pulling on the door and stared at her in shock. "You want to stay in this broken-down place?"

She nodded wildly. "I want to clean it! I know how. I worked for Mrs. Orville. I did everything for her." She swallowed, fighting for breath. "I always wanted to keep my own house!"

Witt staggered backward against the rail. "I thought . . ."

Noelia grabbed the broom in her hands. "I didn't bring this out to sweep with. I wanted to show you a custom my mother taught me."

She waited until he nodded for her to go on.

"When two people want to marry and there is no priest to bless them, it is enough if they hold hands and jump over a broomstick."

Without waiting for him to reply, she reached for his hand. She propped the broom at an angle between the rail and the floor. He followed dumbly, too amazed to question. She led him backward several steps. He could hear her taking a breath. Then she whispered, *"Now!"* They sprang forward.

They leaped! And Witt felt as if he were jumping over the moon. When they landed on the other side she fell into his arms and he held her close.

"Now we are married," she said. The words came as breaths one by one. He felt them as warm forms through the fabric of his shirt. She repeated, "Now we are married."

He clung to her dizzily as if she were a strong young tree

that would support him and keep him from falling. He searched the horizon over the top of her head. There was once again a flat, unbroken line; there was nothing there, nothing scouting for him, nothing riding by. It was empty!

Katie called at six o'clock the next morning, wrenching Witt from a shapeless warm dream of happiness. When he answered, husky-voiced with sleep, she said: "Witt, I need you. Can you come in town quick?"

He saw Noelia's eyes upon him and felt her hand slide across his chest. "What's the matter?"

There was a long silence at the other end. He heard Katie swallow. Then she said: "They're bringing the casket today. I want you with me, Witt. I want you to go with me to meet the train."

Witt closed his eye and nodded. He didn't want to leave his bed. He didn't want to dress and drive away from Noelia.

"Will you come, Witt?"

He nodded again as if she could see him. After a moment he replied out loud, "Yes, Katie, of course I'll come."

He heard her sigh sharply. "Thank you, Witt . . . oh God, I can't stand it! I'm about to die!"

"Just keep yourself together, Katie, I'll be right there."

He replaced the receiver and rolled over to look at Noelia. "I've got to go into town to help a friend."

She nodded and whispered, "I'll make you something to eat when you come back."

CHAPTER EIGHT

Katie was ready when he arrived. She forced a smile for him. A fire burned across her cheeks; her mouth and eyes were swollen. She wore no jewelry, no rattling beads, no earrings, no jangly bracelets clinking at her wrists; so despite the high-necked restraint of her impossibly warm suit she looked half dressed.

She spotted the long Rolls-Royce at the curb. "My God, Witt, how appropriate; pick me up in your hearse!"

The desolation in her half-hidden eyes appalled him.

They circled the depot. The train was late—it always was, but neither had thought to call ahead. They parked beside the vacant platform and walked down the dusty street to the Dixie Grill to wait.

The cafe was almost deserted. They walked past the empty tables to a back booth, followed by the waitress, who had been chatting across the counter with several truck drivers. Her face was hostile, resentful of the intrusion. She turned up the fire under the griddle as she started over. Witt held up two fingers and pointed to the coffee urn. The waitress nodded, granting a smile now that she saw they hadn't come to eat.

Katie worked the glove from her right hand but when

the coffee came she trembled too violently to hold the cup. Witt reached across the table and caught her hand in his. "Take it easy, Katie."

The waitress, back behind the counter, narrowed her eyes and gave her friends a knowing wink.

Witt clasped Katie's hand for a long time, saying nothing, but giving it a squeeze now and then as if he could pump courage into her body. At last she pulled away.

"Are you going to be okay?" he asked.

She gave him a jerky nod and a slight smile.

"Poor Katie."

"Uh-uh," she said, shaking her head. "Not poor Katie. Everything's going to turn out all right. I can feel it."

For an instant she almost relaxed, believing herself. She reached bravely for her cup. Suddenly the air around them was full. A blaring train whistle, two sharp rude cries screamed in their ears. Coffee splashed onto the table. The dark stain spread over the oilcloth and trickled from the edges. Witt watched her face crumble before him. He couldn't get to his feet fast enough before the devastation was complete.

From behind the counter the waitress smirked, convinced she was witnessing a morning jag.

Witt hustled Katie out, knocking against tables and chairs, stumbling through the double doors until the two were on the sidewalk. The fresh air made a difference, walking in the air and sunlight from the cafe to the depot. By the time they climbed the steps to the sooty yellow building she had managed to take hold of herself.

The train was already in, spouting steam from its underside. Down the platform an army sergeant stood, legs apart, hands on hips, conversing with Bertram Lee, the town's undertaker. At the far end, its motor idling, its humpback swelling above the raised platform, waited Bertram Lee's black and silver hearse. Its rear doors yawned wide, big jaws to gobble up Wally's casket.

"Howdy, Bert," Witt said.

Bertram Lee turned. He had a way of smiling through mournful eyes. "Hello, Witt . . . Mrs. McIntosh." He touched his black-banded panama.

Witt glanced at Katie. To his relief she looked calm. In truth, she felt calm. Her moment of crisis had come in the cafe when the whistle of the train sliced through her soul like a scalpel, deadening her nerves and ending her pain. Now she was cold and numb.

"The sergeant and I'll take care of everything, Mrs. McIntosh," Lee was saying. "Don't worry yourself about nothing."

Katie seemed not to be listening. Her eyes stayed with the casket, which had been unloaded from a baggage car and was being carried down the platform in the direction of the open hearse.

Lee turned his attention to Witt. "Just bring Mrs. McIntosh over to the mortuary and we'll make final arrangements. I'm sure she'll want the interment to take place as soon as possible . . . considering everything and all." He wanted to be delicate.

Katie's voice struck out of the blue. "I want to see him!"

The three men stared at her in shock. Lee tried to speak again, convinced he hadn't heard correctly. He opened his mouth but the meaning of her words rushed back at him, stunning him into silence.

Witt's hands thrust out and grabbed her arms. "Katie, let these men get on with what they have to do."

She stared past them to the hearse swallowing up the casket. "I want to see him!"

"Katie!"

"I want to see him. He's my son. I have a right."

"The casket's come sealed, Mrs. McIntosh."

"He's my son!"

"The Army . . ."

"Goddamn you all! I *will* see him!"

Bertram Lee's eyes pleaded with Witt.

"Katie . . ." Witt whispered.

"Witt, be on my side! I need you. . . ."

"Katie, you can't. You don't want to."

"I do. And I will!"

With a jerk of his head Witt signaled Bertram Lee to get in the hearse and drive away.

Katie stood fast. She and Witt alone on the platform. Her eyes accused him. "You're supposed to be my friend, Witt."

All at once he felt bitterly tired. "I suppose you'll have your way," he said at last. "Nothing's going to stop you, is it?"

She shook her head.

"Okay." He released her and turned toward the car. "But let me look first. You might want to change your mind. . . ."

"I never opened one of these before," Bertram Lee was saying to Witt. Katie was waiting alone in the mortuary parlor.

"Does she really have a right?" Witt asked.

"Well, I don't actually know." He couldn't control his voice. It quaked with giddy horror. Both men looked to the sergeant, who was sitting unhappily against the wall beneath a hand-tinted photograph of the Lee family funeral plot. The sergeant shrugged and looked miserable. "I never had any experience like this," he said.

Lee turned back to Witt. "Me either. We always just got these boys in and laid them to rest right quick. No one ever asked to view the remains. It don't promise to be a pretty sight."

"Be that as it may, she'll wait out there for the rest of her life unless you let her see him," Witt said.

"Oh, Lord! I *know* people are going to get wind of this and talk. It'll be bad for business."

Witt bridled. "Don't worry. Nothing's going to keep them from dying on schedule."

Lee brightened, encouraged, mistaking the tone. "Well . . ." He wrung his hands and readjusted his spectacles by wrinkling up his nose.

"She'll haunt your doorstep forever," Witt said.

"Well . . ." Lee repeated.

It took Bertram Lee some time to work the seal from the coffin. Witt returned to the shadowy parlor to sit with Katie. While they waited he tried once more to dissuade her.

She answered, "I can't expect you to understand, Witt. You can't know what it means to have a son!"

Like a thin wave spreading up a sandy beach her words, spoken so softly, sank into the heavy curtains and were absorbed beneath the thickness of the carpet. When she looked up Witt still sat on the edge of his chair with his long legs tucked up underneath. His jaw rested in his fingers' bony cradle. His face was unresponsive, unreachably distant. She assumed he had not heard.

But he had.

The whistling silence sang in her ears. It rose high-pitched like locusts on a summer night. She watched him.

Slowly he began nodding, answering her, looking far, far away, seeing Noelia waiting at home. His voice came out of a dream, low like the wind. "You're right," he said. But he wasn't looking at her, not really talking to her. "I don't know what it's like."

Katie couldn't speak. She had never seen him like this.

Bertram Lee intervened by cracking the parlor door. He beckoned Witt with a silently raised finger.

85

Katie half rose from the couch. "You don't have to look, Witt."

He stared blankly. It was a struggle to clear his head. He had almost forgotten what he was to do. Then suddenly he remembered and hauled himself heavily from the chair.

Bertram Lee hovered by the door as Witt passed through. He closed it quickly behind him, jerking his finger to his lips. Witt caught the fierce excitement in the man's eyes above the nervous pumping of his jaws.

"You won't believe it," Lee whispered. His voice crackled as if he had gossip to tell.

"What's the matter?"

"Never heard of such a thing! And I been undertaking twenty-seven years . . ."

"What is it, Bert?"

Lee nodded, as if Witt had already guessed. With a gesture toward the embalming room he said, "Come on. You got to see it for yourself."

Witt followed Lee into the tile and concrete room. In the center was the stark empty slab. On props nearby sat the open casket.

As they drew up beside it, Lee said in a voice of mixed horror and excitement, *"Look at that!"*

Witt slowly swiveled his eyeball downward and stared into the casket. The muscles inside him jerked involuntarily, sucking breath into his lungs.

The casket contained something, but definitely not Wally McIntosh. At one end, as if they had been thrown in as an afterthought, several pieces of water-smoothed driftwood wedged tightly against a whiskery brown coconut. In the center, packed between wadded rolls of soiled and sandy cloth, lay a shriveled, blackened mass of bones, petrified flesh, and fur.

"What in the hell is that?" Witt gasped.

Bertram Lee shook his head until his lips flapped against each other. "I can't get over it! Honest to God, Witt, it looks for the life of me like a dead monkey!"

Witt squinted, amazed and thankful that there was no stench. He examined the object closely. Lying slightly apart against one of the cloth wads was what looked like a waxy, miniature black hand complete with fingernails.

"A goddam monkey, Witt! What else can it be?"

Witt rocked with sudden nausea. He brushed his hand across his face as if he could wipe away the sight. "My God! This will really undo Katie."

"She shouldn't see it."

"She'll have to," Witt said. "Else she'll think we're lying to keep her out of here."

Bertram Lee considered this for a while before nodding in resignation.

Behind them the door swung noiselessly open. Katie appeared gripping the doorknob, her face like chalk.

"*Katie!*" Witt broke away and lurched toward her.

"Let me see him!" she cried.

"Katie!" Witt shouted. "Stop! It's not Wally!"

But Katie slipped past him and ran to the coffin. For a terrible silent moment she looked into it. Then she screamed.

Her legs buckled, pitching her forward. Bertram Lee caught her before she hit the floor.

She didn't faint. Instead a hideous moan bubbled from her lips, a tuneless chant, eerie and horrible. Her head rolled crazily from side to side. Witt wrenched her from Bertram Lee and struck her face with the back of his hand. The blow left a stinging red imprint on her white cheek. The moaning stopped immediately. Her head ceased its wild swaying. Witt picked her up, straining beneath her weight, and carried her from the room.

Bertram Lee flew ahead of them, throwing open the doors to a narrow, airless room with a washbasin and a cot. Witt lowered her to the cot. Bertram Lee shoved a drinking glass beneath the cold water tap.

"To hell with water," Witt snapped. "Bring her some whiskey."

Lee bolted from the room. When he returned with a glass of bourbon, Katie was sitting up leaning against Witt. Her blond hair tumbled in a disheveled cloud around her face. ". . . I knew it. I knew it. I kept telling you he wasn't dead. How could they be sending back his body?"

Witt held her tightly, murmuring over and over: "Katie, Katie, Katie, Katie . . ."

Bertram Lee stood frozen in the doorway.

"Give me that," Witt said. He snatched the glass from Lee's hand.

Katie jerked her head away, declining the liquor. "I don't need that."

"Come on, Katie."

But she refused and repeated again: "I *knew* it . . . I knew it all the time but nobody would believe me."

The sergeant, attracted by the voices, appeared behind Bertram Lee's shoulder.

Katie looked up. "I'm sorry you wasted your time," she told him, "but Wally's not dead."

The sergeant's eyes swung in confusion from Witt to Lee.

Katie pulled herself upright. Witt's handprint on her cheek was losing itself in her returning color. "I was right all along. I knew there was a mistake. I could feel it."

"Oh, *Katie* . . ." Witt begged.

She put her hand over his mouth. "Let's be off, Witt,"

she said quickly. She rose unaided to her feet. "I think I'd like to go home."

At her kitchen door he caught her hand. She turned to face him.

"Are you sure you don't want me to stick around, at least for a little while?"

"I can't thank you enough, Witt, but just now I'd like to be alone."

He shook his head. "Katie, you're going to make yourself sick . . . all this wishing and dreaming that Wally's coming back."

She touched his cheek gently. "A lot stranger things have happened."

And Witt, thinking over the coffin's macabre contents, said nothing.

It was one o'clock. Witt drove back downtown and parked in front of Dr. Koury's office. The door was locked; the yellow paper shade covered the glass panel. Witt knocked and waited. After a moment the receptionist raised the shade and peered out. She had her handbag in her hand. She shook her head. "It's the doctor's afternoon off."

"I need to see him," Witt called through the glass. "It's important."

The receptionist looked doubtful. After a moment's hesitation she said, "Wait a minute," and disappeared into the shadows. Witt stood on the sidewalk rehearsing what he wanted to say.

The woman returned followed by Koury. She opened the door and let Witt in. Then she drew the shade, told the doctor good-by, and departed.

"Sorry to take up your free time," Witt said.

"I'm used to it," Koury replied. He shrugged.

Witt followed him down the hall. A golf bag leaned against the wall by the back door.

"I won't be long."

"Don't worry about it," Koury said. He smiled. He offered Witt a chair and sat down at his desk. "What seems to be the trouble? You're taking the pills, aren't you?"

Witt had to think about that. He couldn't imagine what Koury was talking about. His mind was too full of what he had rehearsed. Suddenly he remember the prescription. For an instant he was tongue-tied, too embarrassed to admit he had forgotten to have the order filled, had no idea in fact what had become of it.

"Faithfully," he said. He paused. "Matter of fact that's not what I came about."

Koury fired up his cigar and waited.

Witt fussed with his hat, dimpling the sweaty crown. He didn't know how to begin. His rehearsal had been in vain. "Doc, I was sort of wondering . . ." He paused. He couldn't keep from grinning foolishly. "What I'm getting at is, could a man my age sire a child?"

Koury plugged up his smile with his cigar.

Witt was blushing furiously. He looked away, avoiding Koury's bright eyes. "I'm asking if it's possible, because if it is I want to."

Koury blew a smoke screen between them and rearranged his face. "How old are you, Witt?"

"Sixty-eight . . . but just barely."

Koury tilted back in his chair and stared at the ceiling. "Well, it's not unknown, Witt. Of course it mainly depends on the woman's age."

"Eighteen, I figure," he blurted out. He hadn't meant to reveal this.

"You old devil!"

Witt chuckled, feeling pride, and stretched out his legs. Setting it in the open put him at ease. "Don't get the wrong impression, Doc. I'm married."

Koury's eyebrows shot up. "You don't say! Who's the girl?"

Witt wrinkled up his face. "I don't reckon you'd know her by name. We've only been hitched one day."

Koury didn't press the point. He knew he'd hear the story from a dozen other sources. "So you're married and you want to have a baby?"

"That's the long and short of it. I guess I've been sour on family life . . . ever since my own turned on me like they did. I suppose that kept me a loner up to now. And I've always been a lazy so-and-so. You might say my middle name's been *mañana*. I've just been poking along through life like it was never going to end. But now I got to think about tomorrow. I'm a married man with a wife that's got to be taken care of. She'll be around a long time after I'm gone. I figure there ought to be someone to look after her. She'll have the ranch of course. It's a godforsaken spread of land, but there's enough oil underneath to keep her right nicely. Still, it would ease my mind if I knew I was leaving a son behind to run the place and keep an eye out for his mama." He shrugged almost wistfully. "I suppose that sounds crazy."

Koury's cigar had gone out. He shook his head. "That's the way people have been thinking for a long time . . . since time began, I imagine."

The two men fell silent. In the hall past the open door Witt saw again the golf clubs against the wall. He replaced his hat. "You got a golf game waiting, so I'll be quick. I don't know any more about the doctoring business than what I see in the papers, but I've read about fancy medicine they have for old codgers like me . . . monkey glands or some such stuff. I was wondering if you might know of something to help me, sort of pump me full of piss and vinegar again."

Koury laughed. "You think you're slowing down?"

"Goddammit, Doc, I *know* I am. A man can't fool himself on that count!"

Koury got up. He opened the cabinet on the opposite wall and took down a jar of pink-colored sugar pills—placebos. He shook a handful into a small pasteboard box. Using one finger, he typed instructions on a paper label and glued it to the lid. He snipped off a length of adhesive tape and sealed the edges. "Here you go, Witt. Take one a day."

Witt reached for the box and gave it a shake to hear the rattle of the pills inside. "You're sure this'll do the trick?"

"As good as anything."

"I don't need a shot or monkey glands or anything like that?"

Koury smiled. "Stick to these for a while and let's see what happens."

"I'm counting on you, Doc."

"I've done my part, Witt. The rest is up to you."

Witt grinned. "Hell, Doc, I'm going to do my damnedest!"

Koury laughed out loud. This was worth delaying his golf game. He gave Witt a pat on the back.

"What do I owe you?"

"Keep your hand out of your pocket. Call it a wedding present from me."

Witt was astonished . . . and touched. "Goddamn, Doc! Pills like these must cost a pretty penny. I can afford it, why don't you take my money?"

"Forget it, Witt."

"I'm real grateful. I want you to know that. And one of

92

these days, when I see the chance, I'll find a way to thank you properly."

Koury nodded. He reached for his golf bag and edged Witt toward the back door. "Go on home to your wife and put those pills to a test."

Witt headed out of town in high spirits. As he caught sight of the solitary ranch house on the horizon, he fished the pasteboard box from his shirt pocket. He steered with his knees while he stripped the tape from the lid and jauntily popped one of the pink sugar pills into his mouth.

"*Whoopee!*" he shouted jubilantly, and stepped on the gas.

CHAPTER NINE

Witt hired a crew of carpenters to remodel his ranch house from the ground up. The workmen went back to Landry after their first day on the job with the gossip that Santa Noelia had run off with Señor Witt. The news reached Betty Jean Schneider's ears the next morning during coffee break at the drugstore across from the bank. It was the juiciest story she'd heard since Judge Smokey Matthews fell off his bench in the middle of a trial dead drunk.

She couldn't believe her luck when she returned to her teller cage and found Roseanne standing at the end of the line. Out of the corner of her eye she watched with malicious delight as Roseanne carried on, acting like a heavy depositor. She was sighing out loud, craning her neck every second or two to count the people ahead of her, and impatiently tapping a trail of cigarette ash on the floor as she inched forward.

Betty Jean's fingers flew. Bills snapped into neat stacks, coins vanished with a tinkle into the money tray, the rubber stamp whomped its inky blue imprint on deposit and withdrawal slips. She was as impatient as Roseanne to get rid of the customers between them.

94

At last Roseanne stepped up. She clamped her lips into a hard line, ready to complain about the long wait.

Betty Jean never gave her the chance. Her voice thundered above the hum of business and clackety-clack of typewriters and adding machines. It boomed to all parts of the lobby. "Why, howdo, Roseanne! What's this I hear about Witt playing house with a little Mexican girl?"

Roseanne's purse crashed to the floor.

"Did I get the story wrong?" Betty Jean roared. The bank went dead silent. All eyes glued to Roseanne's startled face. "I heard that the Sanchez girl, the one that saw the vision, just up and ran off with your brother. They're supposed to be living together in front of God and everyone out at his place."

"Hush your big mouth, Betty Jean, or I'll scratch your eyes out!"

The teller's voice shifted to a stage whisper. "Lordie, Roseanne, don't tell me you haven't heard? You must be the last person in town!"

Roseanne flushed, veins swelling in her thin neck. Over the rustling snickers behind her someone said out loud: "Talk about Daddy and Peaches Browning!" There was a chorus of lewd laughter.

For a long humiliating moment Roseanne was too mortified to move. She stood stock still, gripping the cold marble counter edge, staring at Betty Jean as if she were gazing at the Gorgon.

This was too much to bear—Witt had finally dragged the family name too low. A Tyler, her own brother, living blatantly with a common Mexican girl! She couldn't stand it: people laughing and talking behind her back.

She snatched her purse off the floor and stalked out.

95

Five minutes later she was at home, so addled she could hardly hold the telephone.

She never gave Floyd a chance to finish his hello. "Have you heard about Witt?"

"Is he dead?"

"I wish to hell he was!" The story poured out, so scrambled with invectives against Betty Jean and the men who snickered around her that Floyd had to ask her to repeat it. When she finished for the second time he had a vague idea of what had happened.

"He never was much good."

There was a moment's incredulous silence at Roseanne's end. "Is that all you can say?"

"What am I supposed to say?"

"For Chrissake, Floyd, you're a man of God. Seems to me you'd be raring to go out there and break up their little love nest!"

The very thought appalled him. "I couldn't do a thing like that, Roseanne. I haven't spoken two words to Witt in twenty years."

"You drive me to distraction, Floyd! It's plain as day you don't give two hoots for the family's good name."

"Phooey, that's not what's eating you. I expect you're a lot more worried about tattletale gossip."

The truth stung. "I never gave such a thing a passing thought, but since you insist on bringing it up I hope you're going to be able to hold your head high in the pulpit knowing what all those people out there are thinking and saying. My pew will be empty, you can count on that. I'm so embarrassed I don't dare poke my face out of the house."

"Now, Roseanne . . ."

"The very idea, the preacher's own brother robbing the cradle, carrying on with a Mexican *puta*. If you need a

96

sermon topic you might think about the Seventh Commandment."

Her taunting raised Floyd's hackles. "Better yet, Roseanne, maybe I should talk about casting the first stone."

The phone clicked dead in his ear.

The story finally made its way out to the Orvilles' farm. The news that Noelia had run off with a man sent Carmen flying from the house wailing with rage. Hector chased into the barnyard after her and shook her into silence. "What's so bad, after all?" he shouted at his wife. He was delighted his daughter had finally left. Besides, it was no worthless lay-about she had run off with. *"Un Señor!"* he reminded Carmen, speaking the words with exaggerated respect. "Witt Tyler is *un Señor.*"

Carmen reluctantly conceded to the title's prestige.

"Un Señor," Hector repeated, seeing her soften. "Rich, with his own *hacienda.*" He let the significance of Witt's ranch sink in. She followed his eyes on a tour of the ravaged barnyard about them.

Putting the farm in order again was going to take more than what overflowed Mrs. Orville's zinc washtub. And neither Carmen nor Hector had missed the farmer's accusing narrow-eyed stares and barbed remarks. It was plain where he laid the blame for the disaster. Furthermore, he had been away all day and Hector was convinced he was scouting the area for a man to take his place. When Mr. Orville came up with his new worker, the Sanchezes would have to pack up and look for another place.

"Sí, sí," Carmen muttered, picking her way through the debris that littered the ground. She could feel Mrs. Orville's baleful eyes on her back, burning from the kitchen window.

"The Lady must have sent such a *señor* to Noelia . . . and it is true he has a big *hacienda.*"

Roseanne holed up in seclusion at home, her ears burning. The further news that the entire Sanchez family had moved lock, stock, and barrel onto Witt's place, lodged in two mobile trailers beside the ranch house, only intensified her chagrin. She was seen only once, a brief, icy appearance at the bank to transfer her account elsewhere. The look in her eyes was calculated to turn Betty Jean Schneider to salt. Her expression beneath the tight fringe of red hair was stony, concealing what swirled within her brain as white fury.

Possom toured around town like a lost soul, staying out as late as he dared, dreading the return home, where Roseanne always seemed to be. With nothing else to do, she was making his life more miserable than ever, grilling him every time he slinked in the back door: "Possom, are you toeing the line?"

Making a beeline for the liquor cabinet he would sigh, "Honest to God, Roseanne, I never walked so straight in all my life."

It was the truth. It seemed impossible to do otherwise. The profit he cleared after delivering the pipe would have burned a hole in his pocket, but Roseanne had snapped up the money, repaid the loan, and deposited the rest in her own name. "Possom," she announced. "You're not only on vacation, you're out of business altogether."

He haunted the Main Street cafes, horning in on everybody's coffee breaks, trying to smile through his hangdog look, choking back his shame at being out of work. And when the cafes emptied during the lonely hour before lunchtime he would pull out a well-thumbed copy of *Reader's Digest* and flip through the pages to the article that was setting his imagination on fire.

For the hundredth time he mouthed the title silently, licking his lips with excitement: "Uranium! How It Can Make You a Millionaire!"

"Imagine that!" he said to himself. "All that uranium lying around undiscovered with the government itching to pay top dollar for it . . . and nobody around here is lifting a finger to cash in. Christ, it's like a license to print your own money!"

Money! The one thing he didn't have. How could he cash in on the uranium boom without two cents to rub together?

Above the pounding hammer blows and whining saws, Witt's ears picked up the approaching rumble of a delivery truck on the newly paved road outside his house. He had been marching among the carpenters like a general inspecting troops. For days he had been supervising every driven nail, every tile, every shingle that replaced the old in the transformation of his house.

The truck pulled up at the end of the new flagstone walk and stopped. Witt left the carpenters and sought out Noelia.

"Come outside with me, honey," he said when he found her. "I've got a present for you."

She clapped her hands. "Oh, Señor, what is it? Tell me!"

His eye sparkled. "Hold your horses. You'll see."

She ran ahead of him down the steps. Two men were struggling with a long, oblong crate, obviously heavy. They lowered it gingerly from the truck bed.

"Uncrate it here, boys," Witt said as he drew near.

The men produced crowbars and pried apart the yellow slats, baring the object packaged in brown paper. Noelia danced with excitement.

Witt held up his hand. "Let the lady unwrap it. It's her new toy."

Noelia squealed as she jumped forward and began tearing

99

at the paper. The wrapping fell back to reveal an enormous bathtub, pink marble shot through with white and gold like a cloud-streaked summer sky at sunset.

"*Aiiii, Señor!*" she screamed. She jumped inside, running her palms over the gleaming-wet-like stone.

Witt grinned. Her joy delighted him.

She reached up, mischief-eyed, and tugged at his hands.

"Hey, whoa, whoa!"

She laughed, teasing him. "Come on, Señor. Get in too. It's plenty big for both of us!"

His knees bent. With an embarrassed giggle he slipped sideways into the tub beside her. His long legs dangled over the side to the ground.

The delivery men were too surprised to look away. They watched as Noelia wrapped her arms around Witt's neck and kissed his cheek. "Señor," she whispered in his ear, "it's just what I always wanted."

CHAPTER TEN

On Sunday, about two weeks later, Noelia rose a few minutes before seven and dressed to join her family for church. She dropped her rosary around her neck, covered her head with a mantilla, and tiptoed silently from the bedroom in order not to awaken Witt.

But he heard every movement. He had been awake for hours, unable to move.

He lay, sunk deep in his pillow, staring with a frightened, pale eye at the blankness of the ceiling, trying to understand what had happened to him. His mind reeled with confusion. He figured that sometime during the night he had suffered a stroke. Whatever it was, it had pinned him helpless to the bed since four o'clock, disorienting him, leaving him unsure of the exact location and deployment of his arms and legs. His tongue seemed to fill his mouth, a flaccid, lolling lump against his teeth. With every quick, shallow breath a bubble of saliva formed, grew, and burst with a little pop at the corner of his lips. After she left, he managed enough co-ordination to suck it back in. But for a long time that was the most he could do.

The morning sunlight inched across the ceiling. As it progressed, crawling with maddening slowness, Witt began to recover. Sweat filmed his forehead. It filled the deep creases and seeped into the tangles of his hair. His teeth clattered together though he felt quite warm.

Gradually he sensed life returning to his limbs. He took a breath and tried moving his fingers. Their response was feeble and spastic, but he almost cried with relief. They flexed with growing discipline as he worked his fists open and closed. Then he raised his arms, bringing them toward his chest and dropping them back at his side. The exercise exhausted him. He rested, breathing hoarsely, for nearly an hour before attempting to sit up.

As he hauled himself into a sitting position, his legs tumbled from the bed and slammed against the carpeted floor. He knew they wouldn't support him. He waited, dying of thirst, sweating profusely, shivering with fright . . . he waited until the sun left the ceiling and began its turtle-crawl down the far wall. Then, using his arms as braces, he raised himself to his feet. He rocked unsteadily, but he was standing. He moved one leg, noticing with alarm that the foot dragged along behind like an atrophied extension. It flopped into place. He stood very still until he was satisfied he wouldn't fall. Then he moved the other leg.

In this halting, careful manner he wobbled from the bedroom to the bathroom, where he filled a glass with water. It streamed down his chin. Laboriously he had to fill the glass three times before enough went down his throat to slake his thirst. Then staring at the ashen, tense face in the mirror he said out loud: "I nearly died!"

The words wallowed from his lazy tongue. As he spoke he felt a chilling shock as if he were hearing quite another person. "My God! I nearly died!" He looked away quickly, frightened by the haunting reflection.

Noelia didn't return until the sun was slanting across the

102

open fields from the west. She had made the usual Sunday rounds with her family visiting aunts, uncles, grandparents, and friends. When she did come home she found Witt sitting on the porch sipping a Coke.

Trailing her mantilla from her hand, looking fresh and strong, she skipped up the walk crying: "I'm home, Señor! I'm home!"

Despite his joy at seeing her after the long, lonesome, frantic hours, he had to force a plain smile. He rose, moving cautiously, and kissed her forehead. She noticed nothing. She sat down beside him and chattered brightly, telling him everything she had done that day. He let her talk on and on as the sun went down and told her nothing of what had happened.

That night, after supper, he swallowed another of the pink pills. But when she slipped her arm around his waist he looked almost mournfully into her dark eyes. He said that he felt very tired and that they "shouldn't try tonight to make a baby."

Katie drove up unannounced the following weekend. Witt was outside when she arrived.

"Katie!" he called happily as she climbed from the car. "I'm glad you came out. How have you been?"

She gave him her big smile. "Just fine. I told you not to worry about me. I never felt better."

"And you look it too, Katie. I swear you're a damned well-preserved woman."

"Oh!" she screamed. She swung her purse as if to hit him. "A hell of a thing to say to a lady!"

Witt shied back and laughed. Katie broke into laughter too and relaxed. "My God!" she said, looking around. "I heard you were remodeling the old place, but I had no idea. It's beautiful!"

Witt flushed with pride. "I stayed on top of those workmen every second. I wanted to be sure everything was just right."

In that past week he had grown strong and well again. He strode over the thick carpet grass showing her around the new lawn. Her high heels pierced the ground like daggers. She had to struggle to match his pace.

"That there is a pecan," he said, pointing into the spreading branches of a full-grown tree. "And over there is orange, grapefruit, kumquat, and tangerine. Back yonder is a couple of date palms, and along against that wall I'm going to set in some banana trees. I don't want anything growing out here that doesn't put out fruit."

His eye swept the blooming rosebushes and confetti-bright lantana lining the picket fence. "Or at least make pretty flowers like those things."

Katie shook her head in amazement. "I would never have recognized the place. It's like an oasis."

"You haven't seen anything yet. Come take a look at what I've done with the house. It's a goddamned palace!"

He led her up the steps beneath an arch of crimson bougainvillaea and into the foyer. As he pushed back the living-room door Katie started to exclaim at the transformation. Her voice caught in her throat.

Noelia was sitting on the floor in front of the flagstone fireplace. She was peering into Witt's old stereoscope, which, along with its double photographs on pasteboard cards, had been unearthed by workmen insulating the attic. The piles of photographs lay in a clutter around her. She looked up at the sound of Katie's voice.

Her eyes darkened suspiciously at the sight of her beside Witt.

There was a fleeting instant of tense silence.

"Noelia, this is Katie," Witt said.

Noelia nodded without speaking.

Witt cleared his throat. "Can't you say hello?" he coaxed.

Noelia complied. Her voice was flat. She bowed her head sullenly. Inside her heart her peasant sense of possession roused the blind worms of jealousy.

Witt gave Katie a wan look, shrugging helplessly. Katie suppressed her smile. She brushed his arm and murmured, "You know, if I don't hit the road it's going to get dark on me. I'm blind as a bat once the sun goes down."

"But you just got here! Stay around for a beer."

Katie shook her head.

Witt frowned, bewildered, left out of the silent confrontation between the two women.

Noelia pretended to be looking into the stereoscope, but one eye peered over the instrument and examined Katie. She found her mass of golden hair very beautiful and envied the jumble of shiny bracelets ringing at each wrist. She hated herself for admiring Katie's bright orange skirt and the yellow satin blouse that strained against her voluptuous breasts. She was scandalized that Katie let the top button go unfastened, showing the dark perfumed crease between them. But most of all she was angry and hurt at the familiar way Katie had touched Witt's arm.

"I've really got to run," Katie said. At the last second she caught herself from touching his arm again. "I just wanted to drop by and say hello."

Noelia ignored her. She popped another photograph into the stereoscope.

"I don't know what got into her," Witt said as he trailed Katie from the room.

Katie smiled. "The green-eyed monster, Witt. You ought to be tickled to death. I know I certainly am. It's the best compliment I've had in ages."

As she started down the porch steps, Witt touched her shoulder and held her back. "Hold up a minute, Katie. I've got to tell you something."

She turned and looked at him.

"Something awful happened to me last Sunday! Katie . . . I couldn't get out of bed!"

Her face had been tight. Now she broke into a grin. "I know exactly what you mean. I've had that trouble before, Lord knows. And that's the kind of thing that can get a person in a fix."

Witt didn't smile. He stepped down until his face was level with hers. "No, Katie, I'm serious! I woke up paralyzed. I couldn't move my arms and legs. I couldn't talk."

"Witt!"

"I'm worried, Katie! I think I'm dying."

"Oh, Witt, you can't be!" She tried to smother the fright in her eyes. "You're King of the Mountain, remember?"

"I'm scared to death."

She sat on the steps and drew Witt down beside her. She tried to speak calmly. "Have you seen a doctor?"

He shook his head sadly. "Not for that."

"Oh, honey, don't be a stubborn fool! Promise me you'll drive in and see him tomorrow!"

Witt stared out at the empty horizon. The sun was coming from a low angle in the sky, drawing saw-toothed shadows from the picket fence across the lawn. In the distance where the oil pumps worked with breathing sighs, raising and lowering their heavy arms, a heat-spawned whirlwind sucked up a cloud of sand from the flat earth and danced toward the whitened horizon. Then as suddenly as it had grown, the spiral dissipated, leaving the column of fine dust briefly suspended in the air. In another instant even that disappeared.

He turned back to her. "Katie, do you believe there's such a thing as Death?"

"What are you talking about?" She studied his face anxiously.

"I mean something real called Death that comes calling for you when your number's up."

She leaned against the newel-post, troubled. "No, I don't believe that." It was a flat statement of faith.

Witt considered this for a long moment. He decided to say nothing about what he had seen moving along the horizon's flat line on the day he first brought Noelia home. He wouldn't mention the icy touch, like a dead man's finger, he had felt drawn across his forehead.

"What's the matter?" Katie said, breaking the heavy silence.

His eye left the horizon and met her worried gaze. "You know the worst thing, Katie? The hardest part to bear?"

She shook her head stiffly.

"I'm not ready."

She started to say something, but Witt spoke again: "I'm an old man. I can look in the mirror and see it. But I still feel like I did when I was twenty. Isn't that crazy? I never knew old people felt like this. I thought they changed somehow . . . you know, got old in their minds as well as in their bodies. I don't mean feeble or senile or anything like that. It's just that I believed they *thought* like old folks, gearing themselves up in some way for the end. I'm amazed when I look back to when I was a kid. I thought all those old people creaking around were different from me. Now I know the truth. All the time we were going around with the very same ideas in our heads, feeling the same about living and loving and dying. Fond of the first two and scared of the last."

"Oh, Witt, hush up!" Katie whispered.

107

"I love that little girl in there," he said. "I don't want it to come to an end. You know, it scared the hell out of me last Sunday when I was lying in that bed, sweating like a pig, helpless as a baby, not able to move a muscle. She'd gone off to church with her folks . . . stayed in Landry all day. I was all alone, just lying there thinking. It's funny, Katie, how quick a person can get used to *not* being alone any more. I can't tell you how bad I felt. I guess the worst part was that I was so goddamned scared that I was going to die right then and there . . . all alone without ever seeing her again. Then some sonuvabitch would come out here and kick Noelia off the place and sell the land to a hundred different red-necks. And in a week people driving by would look out over this dusty stretch and none of them would ever know that Witt Tyler had once passed this way."

A stifled noise from Katie stopped him. He saw her eyes were red and tears had caught in the powdered circles beneath.

"Witt, you make me so sad."

"I'm sorry, Katie."

"I can't take any more."

He nodded mournfully. He took her hands and lifted her to her feet.

"Will you go, Witt?"

"Where?"

"To the doctor."

He nodded. "Yeah. I was too scared to before, afraid that seeing him would sort of put the final seal on it . . . but now I want to go. I got to do something to keep from having another attack like that last one."

"Are you married to her, Witt?" Katie asked suddenly.

She caught him off guard. It was a second before he answered. "Yes."

"Talk around town has it that you're not."

"Well, we're sort of married. It was her idea. I don't know how legal it is."

Katie reached the bottom of the steps. Witt followed her down the walkway. She stopped at the gate and faced him. "Do her a favor. Make it legal. If you love her, that would be taking care of her for the rest of her life."

Witt nodded.

"Promise me."

"Promise."

Katie smiled for the first time since he began talking. She tapped his cheek. It felt like a kiss. "You old dog!" she whispered in her smoky voice. "I guess this means I'm never going to make it to Mexico."

Noelia was watching from behind the living-room curtains. *"Go away, go away, go away!"* she urged in a silent incantation. She crossed her fingers in a primitive hex and directed its power at Katie. The magic seemed to work. Katie opened her car door and slipped behind the wheel. Noelia smiled appreciatively at her effectiveness. She kept her fingers wound in their intricate knot until Katie's engine whirred into life and the car rolled away toward the highway.

As Witt began retracing his steps up the flagstone walk, ambling back to the house, she dropped the heavy curtain into place and sat down on the floor amid the photographs. She intended to show her displeasure over the visit by not speaking when he re-entered.

She gave a desultory glance into the stereoscope, pulling back momentarily to read the caption. *Hagia Sophia, Constantinople; blt. 532–37 by Justinian; dia. of dome 102 ft., hgt. 184 ft."* Her lips struggled to form real words out of the odd spellings and unfamiliar abbreviations. She looked back in the instrument which transformed the pair of flat black and white photographs into lifelike three dimensions. The solidity of the dome enchanted her as did the mysterious way the closer minarets seemed to jump out of the frame into the air; but when she tried to touch them her finger struck flat paper, destroying the illusion. The Winter Palace followed and was replaced in turn by the Woolworth Tower. This excited her, a Woolworth's that big. She was about to drop the White Cliffs of Dover into place when it dawned on her that Witt hadn't come back in.

Grabbing a jumbled stack of pictures in one hand and holding onto the stereoscope with the other, she stalked from the living room in search of him. He was sitting alone on the back steps, his knees drawn up to his chest, his arms wrapped around his shins. He called to her as she opened the door. "Come sit beside me, Noelia."

She gave him a pouty look with her full lips and tossed her hair back over her shoulder in a silent pique. She dropped into a chair on the other side of the porch. Without a word she looked at the White Cliffs of Dover.

"What's got into you, Noelia?"

She replaced the slide with one of a round-faced family of fur-suited Eskimos. The bushy-tailed dogs beside the family sled caught her fancy and she squinted into the eyepieces.

Witt climbed to his feet. "If you won't come and sit by me, at least I can come and sit by you." Noelia smiled to herself as he took the neighboring chair. She considered her point scored.

"What were you doing out here, Señor?"

Witt shrugged. "Just looking at the land." He was thinking of how he missed the old abandoned oil derricks that once straddled the land, looking like black skeletal sentries. Now only the tireless pumps, half hidden in the scanty low scrub and brush, remained behind.

110

"Yep, just looking out over the land." He couldn't tell her he was afraid he was going to die and leave her behind—childless. What a lot of land to leave without an heir! And what a shame to die with nothing left behind to show the world you ever breathed except a flat spread of brick-hard dirt!

"What's so interesting, honey?" he asked.

Noelia peered over the top of the stereoscope and answered, "A mountain."

"Let me see," he said. He took the stereoscope from her hands. When he looked through the eyepiece he couldn't help from snorting. "Noelia, honey, you got to be kidding! Don't you know a mountain when you see one?"

"But, Señor, I never saw a mountain in real life."

"Well, that's no more a mountain than the man in the moon. That's what's called a pyramid!"

"It looks like a mountain."

Witt continued to stare at the Great Pyramid of Cheops. "Only because it's pointy. But mountains are rough and rugged. This thing's got smooth sides." His voice was slow and instructive as his eye studied the pyramid. It grew out of the white sand, its two visible triangular sides burning with the reflection of the bright desert sun against the dazzling, cloudless sky. "The ancient Egyptians built these things thousands and thousands of years ago. That's where they buried their pharaohs."

All of a sudden the pyramid appeared fantastically beautiful to him, an immense artificial mountain that dominated the desert on which it stood. It seemed to shrink even the vastness of the encircling horizon. What marvelous men those pharaohs must have been! What giants to dare to alter the terrain itself to put up mountains to testify that they had once lived as men and reigned as kings . . . mountain builders!

111

And instantly across his rapt, troubled mind the thought came thundering down on him, cutting into his brain like a searing bolt of lightning: *King of the Mountain!*

He was on his feet. The stereoscope tumbled from his trembling hands and crashed to the porch. Noelia shrieked and screamed his name, but Witt was beyond hearing. His eye was opened wide. He was staring with wild frenzy at something on the horizon. Noelia glanced frantically back and forth but saw nothing . . . nothing except the emptiness of brush and sand in the oblique cast of the westering sun.

"Señor!" she screamed again, but Witt continued to stare. His face was transfixed.

The photograph which he had looked at for so long had etched itself into his retina; and now, above the plain he could see rising the pyramid's dark triangular afterimage. It hung from the blazing sky like a perfect mountain peak of rough-hewn slate. It had form and shape, as solid as if it truly stood there from the beginning of time.

In another second the afterimage began to fade. He blinked frantically, reluctant to let it vanish, reintensifying it for another instant. Then its ghostly substance shimmered, more quickly this time, and dissipated like a cloud of wind-blown sand. At last he heard Noelia crying his name. He tore his eye from the deserted horizon and stared at her.

His wild look frightened her. "Señor, Señor! What is it? What's the matter?"

He grabbed her hands and pulled her roughly to the edge of the porch with him. A flush burned across his cheeks. The one pale eye scintillated like a blue-white star.

He knew what he was going to do . . . what he *had* to do as if a divine force had descended upon him and ordained the task. The audacity, the excitement, the magnificence of his plan surged through his body until even Noelia was trembling with the energy coursing through his hands into hers.

"Noelia!" he cried. "Look out there! See where all that nothing is? There, in the middle of that, I'm going to build myself a pyramid!"

CHAPTER ELEVEN

The calendar showed autumn was near. A few impatient trees dropped leaves and rustled dry branches at the blazing sun to remind it that the seasons were changing. Migrants worked till dark picking late crops. Children stayed up late, prolonging the waning days of summer freedom. Politicians started grabbing the check at the courthouse coffee bar, for elections were only two months away. Everyone else rested, exhausted by the long heat. Evenings drew them to their porches with palmetto fans to gossip and drowse before turning in.

Witt and his plan were a pebble about to strike still water.

First came the rumor. Gandy dancers were laying railroad tracks, branching off the Southern Pacific line, crossing Herman Brandt's farm onto Witt's acreage. No one knew why. Not even Herman Brandt. He told his cronies over a beer at the Lone Star Buffet: "He does a lot of pee-culiar things. Maybe he's aiming to buy hisself a train." He didn't tell them that Witt had greased his palm with one thousand dollars cash to traverse his farm.

People shrugged their shoulders, fanned their faces, and wondered. It was still too hot to investigate further.

Then eight growling bulldozers paraded down Main Street,

clouding the air with blue fumes. When news came back to town that they had all turned into Witt's gate, curiosity overcame torpor. A line of cars weaved out of town and pulled onto the shoulder along the property line. The more energetic left their cars and approached the fence. A trio of guards, Witt's newly raised private patrol, reined up on the other side a short distance away. They didn't say keep out, but .45s bulged from holsters on each hip. After a moment, their point made clear, they spurred their horses and loped down the line. The small crowd rested their elbows carefully on the barbed wire, but they did not climb over.

They squinted in the sunlight. Far to the north, across the vast, empty bleakness of Witt's property, the track-laying operation was in full swing. They could see nothing of it; but the clink of mallets on steel spikes stung like pinpricks in their ears.

Their eyes drifted back past the ranch house, all alone in the endless flat plain, looking like a house deserted by a town. Farther on, dwarfed almost to nothingness by the big clear sky, the bulldozers were maneuvering into position.

Roseanne's Cadillac joined the line of parked cars. Possom's fingers itched for the binoculars, but Roseanne kept them locked to her eyes. To appease him she rattled off a commentary: "The bulldozers are lining up like racehorses. I can see Witt, standing out in front. Somebody's with him, a short little character. Looks like Mutt and Jeff, the two of them together. That little fellow is holding up a bandana. There it goes! He's signaling the bulldozers! Jesus Christ, it looks like the Sooner Rush!"

Possom could see that. The bulldozers charged forward biting into the hard earth, stirring up a storm of yellow dust. The engines' roar rumbled across the plain like distant thunder.

In the field the bulldozers plunged toward Witt and his companion, chewing dirt as they advanced.

"Hooweee!" Witt yelled. His hat sailed into the air.

The little man grabbed Witt's elbow. "Hightail it, Mr. Tyler! Them things'll eat us alive." He shoved Witt out of the path a second before the machines plowed past. A cyclone of swirling sand stung their faces, blinding them. By the time it settled, the eight bulldozers had reached the end of their run and were swinging into tight arcs to make the trip back.

The flying sand had whipped Witt's face into a high glow. He spit his mouth clean and slapped the other man on the back. "By damn, Colbert, we're on our way!"

Colbert nearly fell to his knees beneath the blow. He was a tiny man, standing barely to Witt's chest, swarthy, with wild, mad eyes beneath a scowling brush of eyebrows that met above his nose.

Unlike all the other architects Witt had called to build his pyramid, Colbert hadn't slammed the phone in his ear. He couldn't afford to. He hadn't seen the tail end of a fee since making headlines a year back with a scheme to blow up downtown Dallas and start all over. His wild eyes roved as he listened to Witt's plan. A pyramid! A goddamn pyramid in the middle of nowhere! Here at last was a bastard crazier than he!

"I'm expensive as sin," he had warned Witt.

"If I can afford a pyramid, I sure as hell can meet your pissant fee!" Witt yelled back.

Colbert had smiled, a dark scowling smile. He liked that. "I'll catch the next train."

When Witt met him at the depot, Colbert already had the plans. The base, three hundred fifty feet on each side; the apex, a needle-sharp tip leaping over two hundred feet into the air. Its stark, simple perfection dazzled Witt.

116

"I been doing some checking," Colbert had said as Witt pored over the blueprints. "I know a granite quarry you can pick up cheap, just the other side of Austin. All the stone you're going to need. And it's a nice purty pink. Now, if you'd just lay a spur track off the main railroad line. . . ."

Witt did. The quarry was bought. The tracks were already reaching southward, and the bulldozers were clearing the land for the foundation.

Witt broke away from Colbert and chased after the bulldozers, fanning the air with his hat, urging them on like a rodeo clown with an arena full of Brahma bulls. The big machines chugged forward splintering the straggly brush in their path, leaving behind eight gaping swaths of freshly turned dirt. Dust fanned outward in a churning wake. It boiled across the land, swallowing Witt.

Roseanne lowered her binoculars but kept them clear of Possom's reach. "Now, what in the hell do you think that crazy fool is up to?"

Though the question was only a vocal musing of her own thoughts, not particularly directed at Possom, he answered anyway: "I can't prove it, but I got a damn sure good idea." He waited for Roseanne's reply, but when she continued to ignore him he went on: "Yep . . . it can only be one thing. Uranium!"

Roseanne turned and looked at Possom for the first time since they left home. Her bright red mouth puckered into a scornful sour apple. *"U-ranium?"* she said, as if she had never heard the word before. "U-ranium? What in God's name would Witt want with uranium?"

Possom felt as if he had been slapped. "You don't know everything, Roseanne. There's lots of things you aren't up on . . . and uranium's one of them. Else you'd realize the government is paying good money for uranium these days. It's pretty

117

clear to me that Witt's going in for it in a big way . . . all them bulldozers to dig it up outta the ground, his own railroad to cart it away. The thing I wonder about is how he ever knew it was out there in the first place."

"Good grief, Possom! You're the dumbest man I ever knew in my life. Please explain to me, if you can, why anybody rich as Witt Tyler is going to worry about picking up a couple of extra bucks . . . an old man! Just try and explain that to me!"

The idea of anybody having so much money that he wouldn't scheme for more had never occurred to Possom. He scratched his nose in thought. "Well, if it's not uranium, what do you suppose it is?"

Roseanne fixed her frosty eyes on him. "If I knew, do you suppose I'd be sitting out here in the hot sun wondering myself?"

Possom hoped it wasn't uranium. If Witt, with all his money behind him, was going into mining on a grand scale, what chance would his puny operation have, when and if he could wheedle the cash out of Roseanne? Hell! he didn't even have enough money for a down payment on a Geiger counter! He watched the greedy bulldozers chewing their way across the open field. An outraged sense of resentment toward Witt and all his money boiled up inside him. He *hoped* it wasn't uranium!

"Whatever it is it's gonna be big," Roseanne mused as she studied the length of the bulldozers' tracks.

She set the binoculars on the seat between them. Possom snatched them up but never got a chance to look. Roseanne threw the car into gear and squealed back onto the highway. With a scornful glance in Possom's direction she said in the icy voice she knew would shrink his soul: *"U-ranium!* For the life of me I can't figure how anyone could come up with a dumbskull idea like that!"

Possom kept a wounded silence. But he was thinking: ". . . you don't know everything, Roseanne. There's lots of things you don't know anything about. . . ."

The sun was making Witt dizzy. After a few moments he left Colbert alone in the field and retreated to the shade of the porch. Noelia met him at the steps.

"Señor, you're so pale!"

It took everything he had to haul himself up. "Hot as a pistol out there," he said. He dropped white-faced, panting into the nearest chair.

Noelia hovered over him frightened by his pallor. "Do you feel sick?"

He shook his head quickly and fought for breath. "Just hot, that's all. I could sure stand a beer."

She straightened up. Her worried eyes were unconvinced but she slipped through the door to fetch the beer.

While she was gone he touched his left arm. There was no feeling. It was as if he had run his fingers over a stick of wood. He was more angry than frightened. He knew he had suffered an attack like the one before, only milder, much milder. But why now? Why did it have to hit him now just when things were getting started? He swore. His eye swept the horizon. "You're playing games, you bastard! Can't you wait a little while longer?"

Noelia's footsteps sounded behind him. Quickly he arranged his lifeless limb in a natural position across his lap. She came through the door and handed him the cold bottle. He took a sip at the foam that bubbled over the top and sighed. "That's better. I feel much better now."

Noelia sat in a chair beside him. Together, in silence, they

119

watched the bulldozers crisscrossing the field. He found himself dozing off now and again, awakening with a wary jump at the last instant before deep sleep overtook him. Each time he tried to move his paralyzed fingers. Finally, he felt them flex, only slightly, but he breathed more easily. He was going to get over this one, too.

By the end of the afternoon, as the sun hung in the haze on the horizon, he had managed to move the entire hand.

The bulldozers were making their final run. They pulled off to the side and the drivers killed the engines. Silence. Colbert emerged from the fog of settling dust and trudged up to the house. He shook the sand from his clothes before climbing the steps.

"I'm calling it a day," he said. "Be dark soon." He turned and scanned the field. The deserted bulldozers were parked in a row beside the excavation. The evening shadows had filled the pit with purple, like a dark, still lake. He nodded to himself with satisfaction. "That's not a bad ditch, damn near three acres of it. Pretty good for starters."

Witt was barely listening. He was concentrating on his arm. It rose, like a rag doll's coaxed by the shoulder. He lowered it gingerly to Minnie, who was snoozing beside his chair, and stroked her fur. The dog opened her eyes and snuggled in closer.

"I'm in a hell of a hurry," Witt said suddenly. "I don't have time for us to shut up shop every night. Get on the phone tomorrow and scare up some lights. No reason why we can't run this show round the clock, is there?"

Colbert scratched sand from his eyebrows. "It'll mean taking on two more work crews."

Witt snapped his head away. "Hire them."

CHAPTER TWELVE

Colbert might have been half crazy, but he was a good architect and a first-rate organizer. When Witt was satisfied the little man had all the details in hand he had himself admitted to Landry's hospital. He thought he'd be there a day or two. After nearly a week's incarceration he hated the food, underwent every test swearing a blue streak, and drove the nurses wild by refusing to remove his dirty Stetson. Most of all he missed Noelia.

All day he had been lying in wait for Dr. Koury. When he heard the unmistakable footsteps in the hall outside his room, a jaunty clickety-click on the hard tile, he roared through the door. "Hey, Doc!"

Koury peered around the door and waggled his cigar in greeting.

"When are you going to spring me from this horse pistol?"

Koury came in and picked up the chart. "The nurses are pestering me to send you home. They're scared to death of you."

Witt beamed.

"How are you feeling?"

Witt threw his hands wide. "Like a million and raring to go." He was sitting up in bed atop the stiff white sheets with two pummeled pillows at his back. His bony knees poked out of the gaping hospital smock.

While Koury glanced over the chart, Witt took a swig from a Dr. Pepper bottle and wedged it back on the crowded night table between two untidy stacks of *Western Romance* magazines. Then he took off his Stetson and dropped it with casual stealth atop the magazines.

Koury caught the action. He reached across and snapped up the hat. Beneath, just as he suspected, was an ashtray with the half-smoked cigar Witt was attempting to hide.

Koury dropped it in the wastebasket. "I thought I told you, no smoking."

Witt winced, embarrassed. "My friend Katie brought it. I just fired it up to show my appreciation. Hardly smoked it at all, mainly just sniffed."

Koury fixed him with a level stare. "Dammit, Witt, your good-intentioned friends are going to kill you, if you don't finish the job yourself."

"You're talking about that prescription I forgot to have filled." On the first day Koury had wheedled the shamefaced confession out of him.

"Not just the pills. I'm talking about the greasy tacos, the ice cream and doughnuts and hair tonic bottles filled with Four Roses. You're the center of a regular smuggling ring."

Witt sank back in his pillow, abashed. "Hell, Doc, it's this godawful hospital food. I can't . . ."

He stopped. Koury's face was dark, almost angry. He spoke sharply without raising his voice. "Don't you understand I'm trying to keep you alive?"

There was a long silence. Finally Witt answered. "Yeah . . . yeah, I know that. Sometimes I'm a damn fool. I ought to know better. If you write down everything I'm supposed to do, I'll follow it to the letter. I don't suppose I can afford not to."

Koury nodded.

"I promise to play it straight from now on." He resettled his Stetson on his head. Hiding under the brim helped him talk. "I'm building something out at the ranch. You got any idea what that is?"

"Everyone's talking about it, lots of wild guesses, but nobody really knows."

Witt looked pleased. His eye sparkled. "I'll let you in on it, Doc, because you've always leveled with me. Believe it or not, I'm putting up a pyramid."

"A what?" Koury nearly bit through his cigar.

"A pyramid. A full-size honest-to-god Egyptian-style pyramid, just like the pharaohs built."

Koury stared, dumbfounded.

"I know you're thinking I must have gone off my rocker, but hear me out. I'm getting old. I've already frittered away most of my three score and ten and don't have beans to show for it. Even a candle, once it's snuffed out, leaves a trace of smoke behind. The pyramid . . . well, that's insurance just in case those pink pills and all my huffing and puffing don't pay off."

"You really mean it, don't you?" Koury searched his face to be let in on the joke.

"I'm serious as I could be. I've already started." He was disturbed to see Koury frowning. "You think I'm crazy, don't you?"

"No, no. I know you're not. I was just thinking of something else, of the cost of that thing, of how many useful things could be built with all that money."

"Shoot, Doc, nobody ever bad-mouthed the pharaohs on that account. I'm putting it up with my own money, so no

123

one can complain. Once in a while someone's got to do something just for the hell of it, just for fun. There's always people around to put up orphan homes. But who else do you know around these parts who can build a pyramid?"

Koury shook his head and laughed in amazement. He couldn't think of anything to say.

A nurse stopped by the door and called him. He started to leave. He hesitated on the threshold and turned around. It dawned on him that Witt had said it all.

The old man was perched on the bed watching him, looking frail and vulnerable. His long skinny legs were doubled up beneath the smock. The big hat hung low over his forehead. The whitish eye flashed in the brim's shadow like a flickering fire from the back of a cave. Suddenly Koury understood him, the frail cloud of life seeking to prevail.

"King Tut," he said quietly, and left.

The lights snapped on over Witt's ranch. They filled the northern nighttime sky with a milky cloud. The sudden eerie aurora threw Possom into a panic. His pulse raced as he thought of Witt's machinery working around the clock digging up uranium. He felt himself being beaten to the punch, for he was convinced more than ever that that was the only thing Witt's secret project could be. Roseanne's tight fist on her purse seemed to strangle him.

"Money money money money money . . ." he said to himself as he stood in his darkened front yard and glared at the glowing haze rising in the north. "Money money money . . . if I only had a little cash."

His mind raced ahead of itself, thoughts logjamming and bumping into each other in a frenzy to take shape. "If . . . if . . . if only I could lay my hands . . . that Witt's

124

no fool. He *knows* it's out there . . . professionals, I'm sure of it, he must have hired professionals to come down and check out everything to be *sure* he's got uranium."

He shook his head violently to clear his brain. "If I only had the money, I'd sneak around and buy up uranium rights on all the land surrounding Witt's place. Bound to hit pay dirt that way. Where there's smoke there's fire. Then I'd hire my own crew . . ."

"Possom! What are you doing out there?" Roseanne's voice cracked like a whip into the darkness.

Possom could see her shadow sharply silhouetted against the light streaming through the screen door.

"I'm changing the water sprinkler." He stooped over in the blackness, pretending to be handling the hose. He watched between his legs until he saw her retreating from the doorway.

The thought rattled through his mind like a half-remembered jingle: "If I only had the money . . . if I only had the dough . . . if I only . . . if . . . if, if, *if it worked once it ought to work again!"*

The solution rocked him with its simplicity: "If it worked once, it ought to work again! Of course! Oh, Roseanne, you don't know everything! There's heaps you don't know!"

Emmett! Emmett was the answer. If he could be talked into standing in back of a loan once, there was no reason why Possom couldn't get the old man to fall for it a second time. Hell! considering the way they paid back the money, with time to spare, Possom was positive the Corpus Christi banker would be only too happy to give him all the cash he asked for . . . just like last time—except for one small but important change: *Roseanne wouldn't know anything about it!*

Possom took a long last look at the unworldly cloud whitening the nighttime sky. "Better watch out, old One-Eye.

125

Possom's getting geared up to hand you some mighty tight competition!"

Witt had to sit on the horn of his Rolls-Royce before the crowd around his gate gave way and let him pass. As the car glided through, people called out: "Hey, Tyler, watcha buildin'?" "Whatcha got cookin', podnah?" and "How's about lettin' us in for a look-see?"

There was a burst of spontaneous applause. People hanging from the fence posts and lounging on car fenders waved good-humoredly.

He floated past as grandly as a king rolling by in his carriage. Their applause was acknowledged with a stately wave. He left them behind with a mysterious, secretive smile and trundled on down the road.

As he drove up to the house he bellowed at the top of his lungs: "I'm King of the Mountain!"

Noelia heard the car approaching up the drive and flew from the house to welcome him home. He ran up the steps and grabbed her in his arms, lifting her off her feet. "Goddamn, it's good to be home again."

She stroked his weathered cheek with the back of her hand. "Are you all right, Señor? I was so scared."

"No need to be." He spoke lightly, holding her close to him. "No need to be at all. That doctor down there knows what he's doing. Look at all this medicine he gave me!"

He reached into his pocket and pulled out three pillboxes. He tapped each one in turn. "This one's for my heart; this one's for my blood pressure; and this one . . . well, it's some more of those pink pills which are going to help us."

Noelia studied the boxes before burying her face deep into his chest. "Oh, Señor! I was afraid you were going to die!"

Witt shuddered involuntarily and tightened his embrace. "What makes you think I'd go off and do a thing like that? You don't believe I'd leave you here all alone with my business only half done?"

He felt her sobbing gently into his shirt. He raised her face and stared into her eyes. She was trying to smile, but her quivering chin pulled at the edges of her mouth. "Hey now . . ." he whispered. "Hey now . . . don't act like that. I'm back home and everything's going to be okay . . . just like it's always been. Come on, give me a smile. Come on, come on, you're such a pretty little thing when you smile. Show me you're glad I'm back."

She sniffed wetly and smiled up at him, but great, thick tears rolled along the pink rims of her eyes and streaked silver down her cheeks. Witt brushed them away with a knuckle and pressed his nose into her hair. "Oh, honey, I never want to leave you again!"

"Señor! I missed you."

Witt found himself crying, too. He held onto her until he was afraid of crushing her. "You got to be my nurse," he said softly over her sobs. "I'm going to need a little taking care of. It's all written down . . . doctor's orders. Things I can eat and things I can't eat. Same goes for drinking, too, I'm sorry to say. And you're going to have to remember to make me take all these pills. I got to have them every day . . . the pink ones too . . . and I'm just liable to forget one or the other unless you stay by my side and remind me."

"I will, Señor."

"Good." He kissed the top of her head where the hair parted into a fine, white line. When he released his hold on her he saw that her tears had dried. "You know what? I'm hungry as a horse! That hospital cook never heard of salt,

127

pepper, or bacon fat. Let's look over that paper Dr. Koury gave me and see if there's anything in this house to eat that won't kill me."

Later Colbert took Witt on a tour. The excavation yawned deep and wide at their feet ready for the foundation to be poured. Nests of powerful floodlights hung in clusters from a dozen tall poles circling the perimeter. He pointed to a team of carpenters raising a series of low, tin-roofed buildings. "The barracks are nearly finished, couple of days more and the workmen can move right in. I've signed on two hundred to begin with. That hut over there with the chimneys is the cookhouse and next to that is the eating hall."

Witt surveyed the scene. "You've built a little town."

"More like an army post," Colbert answered. He pointed off to the left. "I had the bulldozers clear a parcel of land over yonder, where we can stow the steel beams and stone blocks until we're ready for them. The railroad tracks are coming along fine, ought to reach here day after tomorrow. Once they do, I'll set to work on the unloading platform."

Witt stood on the edge of the excavation with his hands on his hips and nodded. He wished he didn't have to wait. He wished he could shut his eye and reopen it to find himself gazing up at the shining, completed pyramid. He wished he could climb all the way to the top with his head grazing the sky and shout so everyone could hear, "I'm King of the Mountain!"

He turned to Colbert, the short little man with mad dark eyes, and placed his hand on his shoulder. "Just hustle, that's all I ask. The only thing we've got to worry about is time."

The sun was setting as he walked back to the house. The deep blue of the eastern sky paled to turquoise at the zenith

128

before flashing into a golden haze on the opposite horizon, a burning cloud fanning out against the atmosphere.

Noelia was waiting for him as he made his way up the steps to the porch. "Here, Señor," she said. She held out her open hand. Three pills nestled in her palm.

Witt swallowed all three at once. Then he winked, taking her by the hand, and said, "I don't know about the other two, but I got a funny feeling that pink one's starting to go to town!"

CHAPTER THIRTEEN

Possom could barely keep his eyes on the highway. He kept glancing nervously across the car seat at Emmett. The old man had dropped off to sleep almost before they cleared the city limits and was now snoring loudly. Possom prayed the nap would help Emmett stay awake while they were at the bank.

When he pulled into the parking lot three quarters of an hour later he tapped Emmett's shoulder. "Rise and shine."

Emmett's head snapped up. He looked around in confusion. "Where am I?"

"Corpus," Possom muttered.

"Corpus?" Emmett said fuzzily, repeating the word as if he had never heard it before. "Corpus?"

"We're going to the bank again, remember? Just like last time."

Emmett rubbed his eyes, then his long nose and drooping cheeks, and ended up this brisk ritual of starting his brain into motion by twirling both index fingers in his ears. He thought the situation over for a long moment, trying to anchor it to something from the past that would give it meaning. Finally he remembered. "But where's Roseanne? She always comes to the bank with us."

Possom sighed with suffering impatience and said for the

130

dozenth time that morning, "She's home in bed with a sick headache." He didn't bother to remind Emmett that he had explained all this before; moreover, it was a lie.

Roseanne's two-tone green Cadillac hurtled onto Herman and Lunette Brandt's farm, scattering chickens and kicking up dust.

Lunette Brandt wedged a forked pole beneath her clothesline and raised the flapping laundry out of the dogs' reach. Then she went around to the front of the house to investigate the racket.

"Hidee, Lunette," Roseanne shouted cheerily. She had already climbed from the car. "I swan, it's good to see you again. For the life of me I can't recall the last time. You haven't changed one little bit!"

Lunette touched her stiff, graying hair self-consciously. She could spot a bald-faced lie when she heard one.

"Hello, Roseanne," she said. Her voice was distinctly chilly. She remembered exactly the last time they met. A church picnic over twenty years ago, when they were both young and looking for husbands. Roseanne had flirted and coquetted until she had Herman Brandt eating out of her hand. By the time the lunch box auction came around, Herman had forgotten all about Lunette. Mesmerized and glassy-eyed, he spent a scandalous fortune for the pleasure of sharing Roseanne's fried chicken while Lunette fled the picnic ground, blushing with mortification, when her own father had to buy her basket so it wouldn't go begging. For the next six weeks she had waited, in plain-faced helplessness and humiliation, until Roseanne tired of Herman and tossed him back.

Roseanne pranced across the barnyard like she owned the place, flouncing her red curls and smiling brightly. "I hope you're not too busy to chat a spell."

Lunette hesitated for an instant. She had never turned any-

131

one away from her door, stranger, friend, or foe. "Come on in. I reckon I got some coffee on the stove." Her wary eyes checked the field for Herman's tractor. She had no doubt one glimpse of Roseanne would bring him chugging back home.

She hurried Roseanne into the house. With the back of her hand she shooed the tiger cat from the kitchen table and set out two cups.

"What brings you to this neck of the woods?"

"I just drove out to take a gander at the stirrings on Witt's place, and since I was as good as on your doorstep I thought I'd drop in and pay a call."

Lunette gave her a fishy look and poured the coffee. "The coffee is likely to taste peculiar to you. We use well water out here."

Roseanne held her breath and choked down a sip. "Tastes just fine. Don't forget, I was still a farm girl when you were living in town with no idea you'd ever marry Herman and end up out here."

Lunette took silent umbrage at what she suspected was Roseanne's sly way of saying she could have bagged Herman if she wanted him.

Roseanne hurried to the point of her visit. "What's all the activity on the other side of your fence?"

"You mean over at Witt's place?"

Roseanne nodded and shoved her cup away. She couldn't bear another swallow. "I'd give my eye teeth to find out what he's up to."

Lunette was in no mood to be helpful. "Don't look at me. We're good neighbors and that means we don't go prying in each other's business."

Roseanne ignored the remark. "I see he's got railroad tracks cutting across your place."

132

"Herman let him do it just to be friendly." She knew nothing about the money that changed hands.

"Well?" Roseanne said expectantly. Lunette's terseness was irritating her. "Have you seen a train yet?"

Lunette shook her head. "Nope. Can't say as how I've been looking either."

Roseanne appraised her with a sideways glance. She didn't know whether or not Lunette was lying, but she could see she was wasting her time. She poked about for an excuse to abandon her undrunk coffee and leave.

A hoarse whistle lowing in the distance provided her escape. "A train!" she murmured.

Lunette heard it too. She glanced at her watch and shook it as if it had to be wrong. "It's too early for the Southern Pacific."

Roseanne jumped up from the table. "It's Witt's train!"

As if confirming her hunch, the whistle sounded again, two short hoots punctuated by a clanging bell.

Roseanne flew through the back door with Lunette on her heels. Both women ran to the edge of the yard and shaded their eyes with their hands. "Lookie there, Lunette. It's rolling right across your farm!"

It was indeed. Whistle blaring, bell ringing, waving a thick black funnel of smoke, the locomotive swerved away from the Southern Pacific line and inaugurated the newly laid spur. It was hauling some two dozen flatcars, as near as Roseanne's excited mind could calculate, each of which was loaded with massive rectangular blocks of dusky pink granite.

"Look at that, Lunette," Roseanne shouted over the rumble. "What in the world could Witt be doing with all that stone?"

The brakeman flashed them a friendly wave as the red caboose rocked down the line toward Witt's ranch. The spin-

133

ning wheels sang on the shiny new track. Already the whistle was a faint call from the distance.

A troubled frown creased Roseanne's forehead. She turned and stalked back toward her car. "I've got to put on my thinking cap and try to figure out what's going on. Witt's throwing money away like it's going out of style. The more he spends the less I stand to collect when he passes on."

Lunette gasped. She hurried to a half trot to keep up with her. "How do you know you're going to get any of it?"

"Shoot! Who else has he got to leave it to?" She yanked open the car door. "My new Cadillac," she said automatically. "It's air-conditioned."

Lunette never gave it a glance. She was looking over Roseanne's shoulder at Herman's tractor. He had come in close when the train rolled by. Now he had his eyes on Roseanne and was making a beeline in their direction.

"Let go of my door, Lunette!" Roseanne cried. "I got to be shoveling off."

Lunette stepped back, unaware she had been holding it open. Herman's tractor rolled right over a section of fence.

Roseanne charged up her engine, poked the air conditioner into roaring life, and wheeled the car into a wide listing circle around the barnyard. Dust flew from her back wheels. As she dashed past Herman's tractor she fired off two quick honks.

Lunette's whole body quivered with jealousy. "I never liked you, Roseanne Woodley!" she shouted after the disappearing car. "Everybody talked about you! Everybody said you were fast!"

Roseanne reached home an hour before Possom got back from Corpus Christi. When he sauntered through the back

134

door she met him in the kitchen and demanded, "Where have you been?"

Possom could lie very well. He held Roseanne with a steady, innocent gaze. "I've been driving poor old Emmett around. I didn't have nothing else to do. It crossed my mind the fresh air and change of scenery might do him good. But you know what? The poor thing slept most of the time. I guess I just wasted a tankful of gas."

"Where did you drive him?" Not that she was interested. It was just part of keeping tabs on Possom's movements.

"We went over to Corpus to look at the water and the boats. I don't even think he knew where he was. When he wasn't snoring away he kept talking like he was back in the bank . . . you know, where we got the loan." He lowered his voice and opened his eyes wide to add verisimilitude. "It was downright scary. He must have been having some kind of hallucination. Talked out loud, just like he was sitting right there in the bank asking for more money."

Roseanne made a face and said, "He gets worse every day. It's high time Willy-boy steps in and takes over his affairs. Emmett's liable to get into trouble with his mind wandering the way it does."

"Yessiree," continued Possom, buying more insurance just in case Emmett forgot his orders and tattled. "Listening to him talk, you would've sworn he was there in the flesh talking to that banker." He shook his head sadly. "Poor thing . . . I guess to him it was real as life!"

That night Possom slept better than he had in weeks. He had money in the bank . . . a whole cache of money in his own private account. Hidden in the trunk of his car was a block of freshly printed checks, each bearing in the left-hand corner the legend: "ATOMIC URANIUM CO., *F. P. Woodley, Pres.*" Sitting beside them, still packed in its shipping crate, was one *Sup-R Detekt-R Geig-R Count-R.* Before he trundled off to bed, he spent forty-five minutes locked in the bathroom poring over the instruction manual. Despite his excitement he was asleep in less than five minutes, determined to awaken fresh. There were busy days ahead scouting the countryside, buying rights to the untold treasure which he was positive lay unsuspected beneath every farmer's field.

The children who made a game of spying on Katie's house waited out of sight until the postman with the special-delivery letter left her door and drove away. Then they crept single file between the wild woody bougainvillaea and the peeling walls and hunkered down just beneath the curtained window. What they heard did not surprise them, but it chilled the marrow of their young bones—a low, hurt-animal moan that went on and on, a swaying oscillating cry. "That's his ghost," they whispered to one another through chattering teeth. "He must be gettin' her for sure this time!"

Suddenly the hideous moaning stopped. With their fingers to their lips for silence they heard Katie's tortured voice pleading: "Why can't you leave me alone?"

Then the moaning resumed.

The children gazed into each other's knowing eyes and nodded.

People from town continued to drive up the highway to Witt's ranch and line the fence with their cars. The tin-roofed barracks were occupied now, and the workmen who poured into town, crowding the beer joints on Saturday nights, were pumped relentlessly for the smallest piece of gossip. But they were as ignorant about the project as the locals. As near as they could judge, considering the foundation, the steel beams, and the piles of granite, it was going to be a great building. Past that, they couldn't say.

Possom couldn't keep away from the place. Whenever he wasn't bouncing over endless miles of hot dusty back roads, shelling out money to surprised farmers for signing over rights for a mineral they'd never heard of, he was leaning on Witt's fence, squinting apprehensively through Roseanne's binoculars.

It was nighttime. The floodlights threw a canopy of whiteness over the excavation. Possom swore under his breath as he saw Sheriff Leggett's bulky shadow sidling down the fence in his direction. He was bone tired and wanted to be left alone. He had spent all day "sewing up the territory," and it was hard work.

"Howdy, Possom. I thought I recognized you standing over here all by your lonesome."

"Howdy, Sheriff."

"What do you see through them things?"

Possom handed over the binoculars without a word. He was convinced from what he observed that Witt was undertaking some sort of strip mining, pulling out uranium ore by the ton.

The sheriff quit fiddling with the glasses and took a long look. "Powerful gadget here. Puts you right on top of everything, don't it?"

Not close enough for Possom. Off to the left, rising out of the excavation, something new had appeared, something which troubled him, for he couldn't connect it with anything he had read about strip mining. A series of straight steel beams were being erected, just visible over the lip of the hole, forming a line the length of one edge.

Possom was too preoccupied to chat. After a few moments the sheriff touched his hat and wandered back down the fence seeking better company. Possom slipped into his car.

The Geiger counter occupied the seat beside him. Feeling his way in the dark, he tripped a toggle switch and dangled the rodlike detector out the open window on the excavation side.

The machine emitted a solitary click, then remained silent as stone. He pulled the detector back into the car and gave it a rough shake. It had been that way all week—wherever he pointed it—scarcely uttering a sound, nothing like the performance the instruction manual promised.

He dropped it back outside the window. Dead silence. Perhaps he was too far away, he thought. He wished it were still daylight so he could reread the instructions. He felt certain he was doing something wrong. With a sigh of exasperation he hauled in the dangling detector and snapped it between clamps to the lid. "You can't buy a goddamned thing anymore that works the way it's supposed to," he muttered in disgust.

A wave of fatigue overwhelmed him. Thinking he would watch a few minutes more before going home, he rested his head against the back of the seat and closed his weary eyes.

He awoke with a start, terribly confused. His body was stiff. His neck ached. He squirmed upright and rubbed his eyes, trying to get his bearings. The sound of the faraway engines of the working cranes reached his ears as a soft, ominous rumble. He peered around him. The roadside looked deserted in the darkness. Everyone else had given up the watch and gone home.

Suddenly there was a sharp noise of crunching gravel at the side of his car. Possom screamed out loud. A head loomed out of the shadows and poked through the window.

"What in the hell are you doing out here?"

Possom nearly shot through the roof. The voice was Roseanne's.

"Answer me this minute!" she demanded, shaking her finger

138

in his face. "What in God's name are you doing out here in the middle of the night?"

Possom was trembling so badly that his voice was reduced to a weird series of confused, hoarse babbles.

Roseanne shoved her head farther in until Possom thought she was trying to crawl through the window. "For God's sake, Roseanne, use the door!"

"Answer me! Talk sense!"

"I . . . I . . . Oh, Jesus!"

"Possom!"

He gripped the steering wheel for support. "Roseanne . . . I just, uh . . ."

"Do you have any idea what time it is?"

He automatically consulted his wristwatch. "Four-thirty," he read from the luminous dial.

"Jesus Christ, Possom!" Roseanne shrieked. "*I* know what time it is. I was asking if *you* did. What do you think has been going through my mind when you didn't come home?"

"I fell asleep," he replied lamely. The awful trembling was subsiding. He wrestled to collect his thoughts. "I just came out here to look at what Witt's doing."

"I thought you were dead in some ditch or something," Roseanne shouted. "I thought you'd had a wreck!"

"I'm sorry, Roseanne."

"I called the sheriff!"

Possom's eyes grew large.

"Lucky he saw you out here!" Her voice rose another decibel. "I called Seyton and Floyd and damn near everybody before I found out!"

"I'm sorry, Roseanne," Possom repeated. His voice was a pleading whine.

"You make me so mad, Possom," she shouted. She grabbed the door and yanked it open. The dome light snapped on.

139

The car filled with light. Her sharp eyes blinked in the unexpected glare. They fastened instantly on the Geiger counter. "What in the hell is that?"

Possom shrank from the instrument as if it were a hissing snake. "I don't know!"

"Possom!"

"It's a Geiger counter, Roseanne."

"A what?"

Possom's shoulders sagged. He slumped against the steering wheel in misery. The sick smile on his face evolved into a moan. "Oooooaaah!"

CHAPTER FOURTEEN

The bones of Witt's mountain seemed to leap up overnight. People woke one morning, looked to the north, and found themselves staring at the steel skeleton etching a sharp wedge into the sky. They gaped, grinned in astonishment, and looked again. All of a sudden it appeared perfectly natural, as if the big blue sky had always been marked that way. They couldn't imagine it empty again.

That afternoon the newspaper headlines confirmed what they already realized: once the great stone slabs were hoisted into place, Witt Tyler—and Landry—would have themselves a pyramid.

"You fool!" Roseanne threw the newspaper in Possom's face. It was the first thing she had said to him in the weeks since coming upon him on the road.

Possom stared at the article. "At least it ain't uranium he's up to."

"Oh, Christ! Give me strength!" She threw herself onto the couch and squeezed her forehead between her palms.

Possom almost felt sorry for her. She seemed suddenly frail and tired, her thin back hunched in a bow between her sharp shoulders. "What have you done to us? We're getting old when things are supposed to be easy. Oh, God, what's go-

141

ing to happen when Willy-boy finds out you've sold his daddy's ranch down the river?"

Possom was frightened. She seemed to be crying. He screwed up his courage and knelt down in front of her. "Roseanne honey. I'm as sorry as I can be."

She looked up. Her eyes were dry. "Possom, if I could shoot you and get away with it, I would."

He fell back on his heels. She might just as well have kicked him between the eyes.

Her bank statement lay atop the coffee table along with her savings passbook and a clutter of papers blackened with frantically scribbled calculations. She had added and subtracted, juggled and manipulated until her brain and fingers ached; but nothing she tried could alter the stark truth. Possom's first payment was due the end of the month. Throwing in everything they owned they could just squeak by. After that, they wouldn't have as much as a door to keep the wolf away.

Roseanne jumped up suddenly and resumed her marathon pacing. It amazed Possom that she hadn't worn a path in the carpet. She pulled up at the far wall and turned to face him. She was deathly white beneath her red fringe. The rouge on her cheeks stood out in bright circles against the pallor. She gripped her fists until the fingernails cut bloodless crescents into her palms. "My mind's gone dry. I've got to break the news to Seyton. He can't walk on water but maybe he can think up something to keep us out of the poorhouse."

"Possom can rot in jail for all I care!" Seyton shouted into the phone. But that night, whistling gaily, he bounced up the back steps to Roseanne's kitchen and plopped down at the table.

Roseanne gave him a hard stare. "What are you so disgustingly cheery for?"

Seyton bared his teeth like a sly dog. "Oh, I think I came up with something." He dragged out the words, relishing the suspense he was putting Possom through. "I been turning over the possibilities all day, strictly for Emmett's sake, you understand." He jerked his head toward Possom but added as if he weren't around to hear: "Not on account of that moron!"

Possom shrank into his smoking jacket.

Roseanne glared contemptuously in his direction before turning back to Seyton. "Okay, spit it out. What have you come up with?"

Seyton laced his stubby fingers over his belly and leaned back in the chair. "Let's examine this horrific mess logically, from the beginning. Possom's up to his gills in debt, and so is Emmett, I'm sorry to say. No use backbiting, no use harping on and on about the crackpot uranium hunt or Possom's sneaky way he took advantage of Emmett . . . what's done is done. I can't bail them out and neither can Floyd. That leaves us with only one person around here with the kind of dough to cover the loan and get Emmett's ranch out of hock."

"Who?"

"Witt!"

Had she been less annoyed Roseanne would have laughed in his face. "Goddammit, Seyton, I thought you came here to talk turkey! You said yourself Jesus Christ in the flesh couldn't sweet-talk Witt into . . ."

Seyton threw up his hands for silence. "Let's just leave the Almighty out of this. I'm talking about the law."

Roseanne's fingers drummed against the tabletop. Her face twitched impatiently.

Seyton bared his plan. "If we take Witt to court, I don't

143

think it'd be an impossible task to get Judge Smokey Matthews to declare him *non compos mentis.*"

"*Non* what?"

Seyton smiled again like a swain bringing a present. "Senile, in other words, incompetent, incapable to manage his affairs. It's a simple procedure, goes on every day."

Roseanne's eyes grew bright. "Then who'd get control of his money?"

"We're his next of kin, aren't we?"

Seyton rocked on the back legs of his chair, letting the possibilities sink in.

Roseanne's mind was buzzing. "What about evidence? Don't we have to show some kind of proof?"

"Well, of course you do. Otherwise one half the state would have the other half locked away in looney bins. But in Witt's case I don't think we'll have to look too far to dig up something."

Roseanne jumped to her feet and started pacing. "Like that thing he's building out there, that crazy pyramid!"

Seyton nodded, beaming like a schoolmaster with a bright pupil. "Now you're cooking with gas."

"And that little señorita he's taken up with! A man his age! And the train!"

"All grist for the mill, every bit."

"What about the judge?"

"Don't fret about him. I got stories on Smokey that would curl your hair."

Suddenly Roseanne had a horrible thought. "Seyton, you reckon he's going to have any money left?"

"How do you mean?"

"That goddamn pyramid! It must be taking everything he owns to put that thing up."

Seyton sucked at his lips and nodded.

Roseanne stopped her pacing in mid-stride. "I just had a brilliant idea! I think I know a way to bring all his spending to a screeching halt."

"What's on your mind?"

Roseanne gave him a secretive smile. She threw her shoulders back, hands on hips, and forced her breasts against the fabric of her blouse. "You take care of Smokey and leave the rest to me. I know just the right person to work my charms on."

Seyton swallowed uneasily, but smiled. Possom scowled from deep within his smoking jacket.

Herman Brandt grinned with pleasure as he recognized Roseanne's Cadillac. He could hardly believe it when the car ground to a stop on the caliche roadside along his fence. He diverted his tractor, ignoring the swath he was cutting across the freshly turned furrows. When he reached the fence he jumped to the ground and scrambled through the barbed wire. With a pretty smile Roseanne reached across the front seat and threw open the door.

"Hidee, Herman," she yelled over the engine roar. "Hop in!"

Herman displayed his grimy overalls. "Don't wanna mess up that fancy car, Roseanne. I'm covered tip to toe with dirt and sweating to beat the band."

"Hurry up, Herman," she snapped, momentarily forgetting her charm, "can't you see you're letting all my cold air out?"

Herman thoughtfully spread his wrinkled bandana over the seat and obeyed. "Never been in an air-conditioned auto before," he said.

"The very first one in Landry, I'm proud to say," she explained, all smiles again. Herman's Adam's apple bobbed nervously up and down his long neck.

He hadn't been this close to her in years. He recalled when they both were young, when her flirty eyes snubbed a row of disappointed young men holding up the wall in the Fourth of July stag line and fixed on him. Enticing eyes, flashing with yellow flickers from the swinging Japanese lanterns. His heart had flown into his throat, thumping so violently that he couldn't speak.

He peeked at her shyly. Even after all these years he could still feel a souvenir flutter against his ribs. His throat tightened and went dry. He remembered how she had locked her fingers in his and lured him into the unlighted storeroom behind the bandstand. The chorus of "Bye, Bye, Blackbird" boomed through the beaver-board wall and rattled the floorboards where they lay, but Herman could still hear Roseanne's excited, high-pitched giggles.

He felt a surge of hot blood filling his cheeks, bringing his sallow skin to a rosy blush. He remembered walking home alone afterward to his father's farm. The warm summer night's air was cool against his burning face. A startled owl hooted at him from a tree's dark branches, a feeble sound compared to the drumming in his ears. The dirt road had been a fleecy cloud beneath his feet. He could still hear his earnest, boyish voice as he floated along in the dark: "Now I know Roseanne better than I've ever known any other girl . . . and that pretty thing knows me better than she knows any other man." He was dead wrong in this assumption, as far as Roseanne was concerned, but he was too young and too green to know any better.

Roseanne moved in on his memories. "Guess you're wondering what I'm doing out here."

"Huh?" He blushed even more deeply as he became conscious of his private thoughts. He wiped his hands over his face, pushing them guiltily aside. His dirty fingers left an oil smear, like a cartoon mustache, beneath his nose.

Roseanne read the nervous gesture: she knew, even before she started, she was going to get her way. "You see," she began, speaking softly, playing the scene, "it's poor, old Witt. I hate to say it, but it ought to be plain as day. He seems to have gone and lost his mind."

Herman's eyes left hers for a moment and darted to the horizon, where the pyramid's dark girders pushed against the sky.

Roseanne waited until she had captured his attention once again. "He's about to run through his fortune building that monstrosity over there. Bad as he's acted all these years, Seyton, Floyd, and me just can't bring ourselves to sit back and watch him throw everything away out of folly. Especially now that he's old and . . . and senile."

Herman wondered why she was telling him all this. "He's always been a little funny," he said in a solemn, sober voice.

Roseanne edged nearer to him, just close enough to raise the fire into his cheeks again. "I'm so glad you noticed, Herman, because I need your help. The only way we can see to keep him from squandering every last cent he owns is to cut off his building supplies. You can do that, Herman, for us and for Witt . . . if you go to the depot and tell them you don't want that train crossing your property any more."

She reached out and touched the frayed cuff of his sleeve. He shivered as if she had stroked him with a branding iron. He swam into her eyes.

In her yard Lunette stood paralyzed with anger, a clothespin clenched between her grinding teeth. She didn't budge until she saw Herman's distant figure re-emerge from Roseanne's car and climb back through the fence. Then, hanging up the last dripping towel to dry, she stalked furiously back to her house and bolted shut both doors from inside.

In the meantime Seyton was paying a call on the county judge. Smokey Matthews was sitting in his chambers behind his mahogany desk. He was stripped to his shirt sleeves with a damp handkerchief stuffed into his open collar. He fanned himself with a pleated sheet of courthouse stationery.

"Terrible warm, ain't it?" he said in greeting as Seyton poked his head around the frosted glass door.

"You alone?" Seyton whispered before entering further. Like a conspirator, his eyes swept the room.

"What's up?"

Seyton eased the door shut behind him and slumped into the leather chair across the desk.

Smokey Matthews dropped the limp fan into the wastebasket and sponged his forehead with the damp handkerchief. Seyton detected the flicker of interest in his friend's hooded eyes. "Family problems," he said.

"Oooh?" Smokey said, drawing the word out with a long rising breath.

"Afraid so." Seyton tried to sound mournful. "Yep, we got a family problem looming up plain as day, and I figured I'd better talk it over with you before jumping in whole hog. You sure we're alone?" He eyed the open door to the secretary's office.

"Clara's out to coffee. Ain't nobody here except you and me." Smokey leaned forward, itching to learn what was behind Seyton's mysterious caution.

Seyton met him halfway, resting his elbows on the glass-topped desk. He said in a voice barely above a whisper, "Just between you, me, and the fence post, the family's considering NCM proceedings."

Smokey was disappointed. He had hoped for more exciting gossip. He relaxed back in his seat. "I ain't a bit surprised. I been wondering when you all'd finally get around to it. Poor old thing hasn't been right in years. Plain as the nose on his face to anybody that sees him. Damn shame what this getting-old business does to you, real sad stuff."

Seyton sighed with relief. He only half heard what Smokey said next: "I guess you'll have Willy-boy take out the papers."

"What?" Seyton asked, suddenly bewildered.

"I just said, I expect Willy-boy'll initiate proceedings . . ."

Seyton was sitting up straight by now. "What in the world does Willy-boy have to do with it?"

"Well, hell, it's his pa, Emmett, you're talking about, ain't it?"

Seyton's pink face grew red. "Hell no, man! I wouldn't do nothing like that to Emmett in a million years."

"Well then, who *are* you talking about?"

"Witt, of course."

Smokey stared at Seyton in surprised silence for a long moment before taking a fresh sheet of stationery from his top drawer and pleating it into a new fan. He batted the warm air around his damp face, then started nodding slowly.

Seyton sucked nervously at his lips, waiting for Smokey to speak.

Finally Smokey said, "What do you know . . . Witt! I plumb forgot about him."

"Well . . . ?" said Seyton.

"Well, what?" Smokey replied, fanning rapidly.

"Well, what's your opinion? You'll be hearing the case, won't you?"

"Reckon I will," Smokey answered. "You got some other judge in mind?"

149

Seyton shifted uneasily in his chair. "I was just wondering if you'd be sympathetic."

Smokey frowned, feigning offense. "I'm impartial, Seyton. You know better than ask me that. I got no opinion one way or the other until I hear the facts."

"Hell, I'm aware of that. I was just fishing to see if you'd be opposed."

"I ain't opposed, if that'll set your mind at ease. But that don't necessarily mean I'm *for*. Just like I said, I got no opinion yea or nay."

Seyton was disturbed by Smokey's ambivalence. He started to rise, then hesitated, deciding to apply a little muscle. "How's the campaign shaping up? Scuttlebutt around town has it this year's election is liable to be a horse race."

Smokey kept on fanning. "I ain't particularly worried. I been winning for twenty-five years. I ain't counting on retiring just yet."

Seyton paused, then dropped his ace on Smokey's desk. "How's the road coming along?"

Smokey's fan never missed a beat. "What road you talking about?"

Seyton clapped his hand over his mouth as if he had let slip a secret. "Ooops, I got to learn to keep my mouth shut. I guess no one's supposed to know about it yet. Fact is, the county commissioner dropped by the house last week. Unless I'm mistaken he sort of inferred the county was going to build a new road to link up the two highways. The way I gathered, it's going to mee-ander all over the countryside instead of cutting right across the way a person might expect. First, it's going to bend a little one way till it skirts past the front of his farm. Then it's going to make another little twist and run alongside your place. Mighty lucky for you, I'd say."

Smokey avoided Seyton's look and concentrated on rearrang-

150

ing the damp handkerchief inside his open collar. He spoke with careful nonchalance. "I don't know beans about it. My business is judging, not road building."

Seyton nodded innocently. "I was sure you didn't. And I won't breathe another word about it. If a nasty little rumor like that got talked around there's no telling the amount of mischief it might stir up. People like to believe the worst. They're liable to imagine you and the commissioner are in cahoots on a bit of hanky-panky. Talk like that could change a vote here and there."

"My nose is clean."

Seyton nodded gravely. "Always has been, Smokey. I been telling people that for years . . . no matter what they say to the contrary." He gave him a sideways smile and stood up. When the door shut behind him, Smokey threw his paper fan into the wastebasket and mopped his face. "Goddamn two-bit shyster! Don't he know blackmail's against the law?" He wondered angrily how much liquor Seyton had poured down the commissioner to wheedle out that bit of information.

CHAPTER FIFTEEN

Peace and quiet was all Dr. Koury wanted, a few unbothered minutes away from the nagging telephone, free from patients' questions and minor complaints that could have waited until he was in his office the next day. Already they had cost him an hour and a half of his afternoon off. Expertly he eased a patient off the line, hung up, and slipped quickly outside before the ringing phone caught him again.

He strolled happily through the orange trees in the grove behind his house. Yellow jackets buzzed around the dark leaves. Their wings flashed like silver disks in the sunlight. The air was warm and still, filled with the tart fragrance of ripe citrus. For a moment he was at ease.

Then he spotted Roseanne.

She came stalking ankle-deep through the high grass. He tried to hide behind a tree. Too late. She was shaking her curls and waving. "I swan, Doc, you're a hard man to get hold of!"

He removed his cigar and nodded. "You can find me in the office six days a week, sometimes seven."

She screwed up her face. "Lordie, a person could spend half his life waiting in your reception room. I got a dozen better ways to waste my time. I figured I'd just catch you here when you had a free minute."

Koury sighed.

She followed him through the orange grove and plucked a waxy leaf and began shredding it methodically to its stem with her bright red fingernails. "I came to talk about Witt," she said.

Koury was examining the yellow fruit that hung from the trees. He picked two ripe oranges, letting the branches spring back, and turned to face her. His raised eyebrows told her he was listening.

"We're concerned about him, as you might expect. We think old age has finally caught up with him. Seyton and me have done a little talking and we've come to the conclusion that it's time someone stepped in and took over his affairs."

Koury said nothing.

Roseanne worked her mouth into a smile. "Naturally we're going to need a doctor's opinion when we take him into court. Since you've been treating him off and on lately we figured you know the score."

Koury chewed on his cigar and walked to the edge of the grove. Through a parting in the trees and shrubs he glimpsed the faraway pyramid's lacy girders against the sky. "What makes you think he's incompetent?"

Roseanne scoffed and caught up with him. "Hell's bells, Doc! Lookie yonder. No man in his right mind sets out to build a pyramid!"

"Is that a fact?" Koury said in a tone of surprise. "What about the pharaohs?"

She tossed back her head and screamed delightedly.

"What about the Indians in Mexico?"

She stopped laughing. "You being funny, Doc?"

"No . . . I'm not trying to be."

153

She stared at him. Her face was set hard, her eyes challenging, her jaws pumping. "You mean you think Witt's carrying on like a sane man?"

Koury's eyes settled once more on the spidery outline above the horizon. "I'm saying that he's simply doing the same thing other men have been doing or dreamed of doing since the beginning of history."

"Building pyramids?" Her voice was incredulous.

"Pyramids, statues, books, sons, and heirs. It all boils down to the same thing."

She threw up her hands in dismay. "I can't believe I'm hearing correctly. Are you saying you can't see your way clear to tell the judge Witt's slipped off the deep end?"

"That's right. I think Witt knows exactly what he's doing."

She rolled her eyes to the sky, fluttering her lids. Then she shrugged, lifting her chin with a defiant jerk. "Well, I guess that means we'll have to go to the trouble of finding ourselves another doctor. Five'll get you ten we can get another opinion even if it takes a court order to drag Witt to a mental exam."

"Why don't you leave the old man alone, Roseanne?"

She scorned the question with a flick of her hand. "Cause he needs help, as any fool can plainly see."

Koury bit down on his cigar. She saved him the unpleasantness of throwing her off his place by turning with a flounce and marching away.

His refusal to collaborate didn't bother her. It wouldn't matter even if he took the stand and argued against them. Seyton could enlist another doctor easily enough. Besides, with Smokey Matthews on their side of the fence, she was sure it wouldn't help Witt if he had the Mayo brothers to speak up for him.

Koury watched her stride back across the grass to her car. After she squealed away from the curb, he rested with his back against the rough bark of a shady mesquite. He stuffed one of the oranges into his pocket and bit a hole through the peel of the other. As he sucked out the sweet juice he stared at the top of the pyramid peeking over the thick hedges. If she gets her way, he thought, the work out there is going to come to a stop. Witt's pyramid would never be finished.

He turned this over in his mind for a long time; then, reaching into his pocket for the other orange, he decided that such an outrage would be a pity.

Colbert pestered Witt for the dozenth time to ride over to the Brandt farm to see what was holding up the train. All morning they had watched its wispy plume of black smoke rising above the horizon at the far side of Herman's land. At first sight of it, the unloading crew had collected alongside the platform ready for work. They waited, smoking cigarettes down to stubs and glancing from time to time to the north, where the rising smoke poured into the sky. It never got any closer.

By noon Colbert had worried himself into a frenzy. More to get the architect off his back than because he believed there was a serious hitch, Witt ordered Hector to saddle his horse, and set off over the prairie to investigate.

He took the ride slowly, letting the horse set its own pace. At the watering hole halfway across he paused and dismounted to let the horse drink. While it sucked at the surface of the water, he leaned his elbow into the saddle and surveyed the scene they were leaving behind. The pyramid cut a sharp inverted V against the cloudless sky. By looking at its base, where the third row of stone was nearly complete, he could carry the granite on up the sloping sides, mentally fleshing out the bare bones, until in his imagination he foresaw the finished structure. He gave his horse a fond pat and spoke

155

into its ear, "Goddamn, that makes me feel good. Just looking at it makes me happy!" He wondered if the pharaohs had felt the same joy and exhilaration when they rode into the desert to examine their own pyramids abuilding.

He thought with satisfaction that at last he was on the right track, in the process of doing everything he ever wanted, even if it had taken most of his life to realize what he was after. He had made more money than any man he knew; he was building himself a monument that would endure longer than the town of Landry itself, a true mountain rearing up in sudden, startling splendor out of the prairie's barren dust; and he had Noelia . . .

"Noelia!" He whispered her name and considered his luck. What a funny thing time is, he thought. A handful of years would have made all the difference. If he had been born ten years earlier, or she ten years later, it might just as well have been a million. A barrier more real, more unbreachable, yet more insidiously subtle than any wall or ocean or range of cloud-swept mountain peaks would have kept them forever apart. Then nothing would have really mattered, not all the land, not the oil, not even the pyramid.

When his horse had drunk its fill of the cloudy water, he inserted his toe into the stirrup and swung back into the saddle.

A nagging worry, one that had been bothering him for days, resurfaced amid his thoughts. He was baffled by the failure of the pink pills to do their job. He knew he had done his part. He was trying, God knew. Noelia saw to that. Every night, as they finished supper, after Colbert shoved his chair back from the table and climbed the stairs to his room, she would disappear into the kitchen and return with a glass of water and the medicine. She stood over him while he swallowed them one by one. He always saved the pink pill until last, imagining that by riding down on top of the others it would have a better chance to work its magic.

But there was no denying something was wrong. There was no baby.

He prodded his horse into motion and headed toward Brandt's farm. He wondered if there might be some debilitating ingredient in the other two pills that sapped the pink pill's potency. The thought took hold in his mind. Before he had traveled ten paces he resolved to abandon them for a while, to take the pink pill alone as an experiment. He would give it a week . . . maybe two.

He spotted Lunette Brandt beating a threadbare hooked rug that sagged over her clothesline. She was giving it everything she had, walloping it with furious, mighty blows until it smoked with dust. Witt's horse clip-clopped up to the fence. He called out to her. She didn't hear over the determined thud of the swinging beater. The dust boiled up until she vanished in its cloud.

He swung down from the saddle, looping the reins over a fence post, and climbed over into the yard. At the last moment, out of the corner of her eye, Lunette caught sight of his moving figure. She turned on him with a fierce suddenness, wielding the bent cane beater high overhead like an unsheathed saber poised to strike. The look in her eyes was murderous.

Witt ducked and cried out, "Whoa there, Lunette!"

The beater dropped harmlessly to her side. She stepped out of the cloud of dust. "Oh, Witt! I thought it was Herman!"

She blushed quite red. Witt couldn't tell whether she was embarrassed or angry.

"It's Herman I'm looking for," he said.

Lunette twirled the beater in her hands and shrugged her

shoulders in feigned lack of interest. "I reckon he's out yonder somewhere." She indicated the field.

There was a long, uncomfortable silence. Witt had the impression he had blundered onto something that was none of his business. He looked toward the north. The smoke from the stalled locomotive could be seen rising over the eaves of the house.

"Something's wrong with my train," he said. "It must have broken down. It hasn't moved an inch all morning. I thought if Herman was around he might know what the trouble is. It would save me the ride all the way over there."

"I'm sure he don't know . . ." Lunette began. Her voice dropped abruptly. She glanced back over her shoulder in that peculiar manner that had been puzzling Witt ever since he rode up. She made a face and dropped the beater.

He stooped over to pick it up. "What's the matter, Lunette?"

She looked at him squarely for the first time. "Witt, what's gone wrong with your train just dawned on me. I'm playing a hunch, but I think Roseanne had a hand in it."

"Roseanne? What in the world does she have to do with my train?"

Lunette narrowed her eyes. "So! That's what those two were doing, talking out there in Roseanne's fancy car . . . just as cozy and cute as you please. Ol' Herman, still a sucker for a pair of winking eyes and swinging hips. . . ."

She looked archly at Witt. He understood at last what she was getting at. He said, "So Roseanne's been out here to see Herman?"

Lunette nodded ominously. "Ain't the first time she paid us a visit either."

"And you think she sweet-talked him into . . ."

"Yep," Lunette answered briskly. "Yesterday. She sure works fast, don't she?"

"I'll be goddamned," Witt muttered. "So Herman's gone and stopped my train. Hard to believe he'd do such a thing. We shook hands on it."

"It's Roseanne's conniving behind it, you mark my word."

"I can't fathom her interest in the matter," he murmured. "Part of her silly game, I guess. Lord, that woman never tires of making life hard for me." He looked over Lunette's head in the direction of the rising smoke. A determined glint flashed into his ice-blue eye. "I suppose the next move is up to me."

"Whatcha gonna do, Witt?"

He took a deep breath, hitching his jeans over his hips, and threw back his shoulders. "No Roseanne or Herman is going to keep me from finishing that pyramid. That train's going to roll across this farm if I got to play engineer myself!"

He tapped his hat and started in a sprint for his horse. Lunette spun the carpet beater nervously between her fingers. Suddenly, lifting her chin and breaking into a wide, vengeful smile, she flung the beater into the air behind her. "Wait for me, Witt!" she yelled. "Let me get my horse, I'm riding with you!"

CHAPTER SIXTEEN

The locomotive sat, smoking peacefully, on the tracks just the other side of Herman's property. As they approached, Witt and Lunette could see that the engineer had climbed down from his cab and was standing off to one side shooting the breeze with Herman. Lunette's eyes narrowed into slits as she caught sight of her husband.

"Giddap!" she yelled. She dug her heels into her roan, wishing she were kicking Herman instead.

The horses flew in a gallop. Their hoofs detonated sudden explosions in the gray dust, leaving behind a slowly settling trail of smoke as if they were setting the prairie on fire.

Herman shielded his eyes from the glare. The sun was still high, its light a brilliant dazzle. He recognized Lunette's bobbing figure atop her mare. "It's my wife," he said in surprise. Then he froze. With even greater surprise he realized who the other rider was. "Ohmigod!" he blurted out. "She's bringing Witt Tyler with her!"

He stumbled backward as if he wanted to place the engineer between himself and Witt. The engineer knew nothing of the motives behind that morning's telegraphed message to halt his train; he raised his blue-striped cap in greeting.

160

Witt and Lunette thundered to the property line and reined up spraying gravel.

"Howdy, Witt," Herman said. His voice was a sick whimper.

Witt waited for the dust to clear. Then he nailed him with a piercing glare. Herman swallowed at the lump in his throat. He couldn't match the stare. He quickly shifted his eyes to his wife. She was grinning strangely, unsettling him. He was dancing from one foot to the other. "Howdy, Lunette honey."

Lunette's horse replied with a whinny. Herman's face fell as if he had been insulted. Lunette broadened her malicious grin.

"How do, Mr. Tyler?" the engineer said brightly. He stepped up beside Witt's horse and extended his hand. "I been anxious to meet you ever since I heard about this thing you're building down here."

Witt shook his hand mechanically. All the while his pale white eye remained zeroed in on Herman, who was squirming like a worm caught in a burning sunbeam from a magnifying glass. The charged atmosphere unnerved the engineer. He stepped back politely, robbing Herman of his shield. "Well, I reckon you folks got something to talk over." He retreated a few hesitant paces and then hustled over to the steaming locomotive.

Witt let Herman fidget. Silent moments dragged by. Then he said, "The game's over, Herman. Tell them to get their train moving again."

Herman kicked at a chalky white rock with the toe of his boot and watched it roll beneath a clump of burnt grass. He was trying to avoid Witt's eye. "Can't do it, Witt. Sorry."

Witt didn't answer. The silence was so drawn out that Herman couldn't resist a hurried peek. Witt's eye stung him like a whip. Quickly he looked back down at his feet. Any doubt left in his mind about the state of Witt's mind was dispelled by that penetrating, single-minded, menacing look.

161

Suddenly Herman wished he had thought to ask Roseanne if Witt was violent.

"You better go on back home, Lunette honey," he mumbled to his wife. He had, in the last minute, grown extremely frightened of Witt.

Lunette held her horse firm. "Go on, Herman," she called at him. "Tell Witt why you done it. Tell him who come out here in that fancy car of hers and put the bug in your ear. Ain't no use hiding the truth, because I saw you-all hovering together like two circling buzzards. . . ."

"Go on home, Lunette. This ain't none of your business." So she had seen him, he thought. That's why she locked him out and made him sleep in the barn.

"I'm staying put," Lunette replied coldly.

"Why'd you do it, Herman?" Witt asked. The sinister edge in his voice sliced into Herman's ears. "I'm waiting, but I won't wait long. It's hot and my patience is wearing thin."

"It wasn't my idea at all, Witt, I swear to God!" Herman shouted, cowering between hunched shoulders. "I woulda let you run a hunnerd trains across this land if you wanted to, only . . ." He stammered over his words.

"Only what?" Witt barked the question. It was an order to continue.

"Only . . . Lunette's right. It's Roseanne that put me up to it. Roseanne came out and said . . ." He floundered helplessly and was afraid.

"Spit it out!"

"She said you was crazy!"

Witt flinched.

Herman had backed well away. He was watching Witt carefully for any indication of mad violence, but Witt sat perfectly still.

Herman broke into a babble, as much to end the intolerable

162

silence as to absolve himself of guilt. "She said it was for your own good. She said I had to stop the train to keep you from going broke, cause you were spending all your money on that pyramid. She said . . ."

"Bullshit!" Witt roared. He shot upright in his stirrups, his legs trembling beneath him. "Hogwash! Goddamn lies!" His face went a deep purple. The swollen veins in his neck pushed out and throbbed.

Lunette cried out in alarm; she had never seen a man go that color before.

Witt's nag caught the excitement. It reared nervously on its hind legs, neighing shrilly. Lunette screamed again, thinking Witt had been thrown. But he had leaped from his horse under his own power. He landed on his feet still grasping the reins.

Herman whirled around and tore into a frantic dash across the sunbaked prairie. Both arms shielded his head to ward off the expected blow. He was running blindly. He never saw the fence post he slammed into. He hit it at full speed and it threw him backwards, his arms windmilling crazily. He sprawled on his back, too stunned and frightened to stir. A warm drop of blood oozed from a scratch below his left eye and traced a zigzag through the dust on his hollow cheek.

Lunette clapped her hands together with delight and giggled hysterically. "Hawhawhaw," she screamed, blinking back tears. "Hawhawhaw, God's punishing you, Herman. It serves you right!"

The livid congestion had left Witt's face. He wound the reins around the saddle horn and spoke to his horse. "Go home now. Go on home." He slapped its rump, sending it into an easy gallop across the field. He squared his shoulders, hitching his jeans back up around his waist, and called: "Herman! I'm taking this train through, do you hear? Neither you or Roseanne's going to stop me!"

163

Herman sat dazed, shaking the cobwebs out of his spinning head. He was in no shape to object.

Witt marched off toward the locomotive. The bewildered engineer, who had been watching with wide eyes, scrambled into his cab beside the fireman.

"What's he up to?" the fireman whispered excitedly.

"I think Mr. Tyler just won an argument."

Witt swung onto the locomotive and poked his head into the cab. "Okay, fellows, I'm giving the orders now. Stoke this thing up and let's get under way."

The fireman looked to the engineer, who shrugged helplessly. "Might as well do what he says. It's his train."

"Damn right," Witt muttered, and the fireman set to work.

Witt heard footsteps behind him. He looked around sharply, expecting Herman. He found Lunette. She was standing below him, joyful tears still shining in her eyes.

"Move over, Witt," she hollered. "I always hankered after a ride in one of them things!"

The locomotive coughed and shuddered into life. The pistons plunged and lifted and plunged again. Sparks sprayed backward from the wheels, metal scraping against metal. Witt yanked the cord and set the whistle to screaming.

"Wooooheeee!" he shouted in imitation. He stuck his face into the rushing wind and pulled the cord again.

Lunette was jumping up and down. "First time in my life I was ever on a train, and here I am riding in the engine!" She untied her sash and yanked her apron over her head. "Hey, Herman! Look at me!" she shrieked.

Her words were lost beneath the clatter of the wheels. Herman roused himself out of his daze and looked up. He could see Witt's hawkish face grinning back at him. And Lunette! She was hanging on with one hand, leaning halfway out of

164

the cab. She was gaily flapping her white apron at him like a gloating army's triumphant banner.

Colbert could see by the change in the plume of smoke that the train was moving again. He charged through the work crew lolling around the unloading platform. "All right, time to look sharp. Our train is moving in."

He cocked his head and listened for a moment. The whistle was cutting across the prairie in one continuous scream. "And the way that engine's tooting tells me Mr. Tyler hisself is at the controls!"

Witt stopped the train as it passed Lunette's house. He helped her from the cab. She retied her sooty apron around her waist, still breathless with excitement. "I can't thank you enough, Witt. It's been a month of Sundays and then some since I've had so much fun."

"The pleasure's all mine, believe me. You can ride on my train anytime you get the notion . . . that is if old Herman doesn't take it into his head to put a stop to it again."

Lunette grinned. "Don't you give Herman another thought. He'll be dragging in here directly, whining about that little bitty scratch and begging for something to eat. I intend to keep the doors locked until he swears to leave your train in peace."

"You're a fine woman, Lunette," Witt said in his most courtly manner. "I reckon Herman'll think more than twice before he lets Roseanne lasso him again."

Lunette laughed and backed away. Witt gave her a wave, then climbed back in the cab and told the engineer to get under way.

He brought the train in, beaming with delight at the round of cheers that greeted him. When he told Colbert what had

165

happened, the architect slapped him on the back and congratulated him. Then, turning to the work crew, Colbert ordered them back to work.

As Witt walked back to the ranch house he spotted Dr. Koury waiting for him on the porch. He bounded up the steps and grabbed the doctor's hand. He was still flushed with excitement over commandeering the train. "Man, have I just had one helluva ride!"

Koury shook his hand. "Is that what you call taking things easy?"

Witt laughed. "I don't reckon I'll have to do it again." He added in a warm voice, "Dammit, Doc, it's a real honor to have you visit. Let's grab a beer and I'll give you the grand tour."

Koury frowned. "Not now, Witt."

Witt noticed the worried expression. "What's the matter? Looks like you've got something on your mind."

Koury glanced out across the flat spread to the pyramid. Even unfinished it was a beautiful, awesome sight. The network of steel was knitted together with the complexity of a spider's web. Despite its enormity it looked remarkably light and airy, a lacy wedge. Koury thought of the Eiffel Tower. His eyes traveled down the triangular side to the base, where the rosy granite already stood in rows. Then, as Witt had done so many times before, his imagination draped the open spaces between the beams with a skin of stone. The picture stayed with him even after he turned away and faced Witt again.

"Roseanne came to see me," he said. He glanced back at the pyramid. If he had been troubled before, now he was convinced, as beautiful as it was, it *couldn't* be left unfinished.

"It seems Roseanne's quite a busy lady," Witt said.

"Do you know that she's planning to take you to court?"

166

Witt looked up sharply. "What the hell for?"

"I didn't think you'd heard about it. She and Seyton want to have you declared legally incompetent."

Witt's eye opened wide. He nearly laughed out loud. "Let them try! They don't have a prayer!"

Koury held up his hand. "Hold on a minute. When I told her I wouldn't have any part in testifying against you, she talked about getting a court order. They can force you to undergo psychiatric testing."

"She must be kidding! Hell, I'm saner than both of them put together."

"She doesn't think a man in complete control of himself would be building a pyramid. Face it, she won't have to look far to find a psychiatrist who'll agree with her. Anyway, it will be a long, hard ordeal."

Suddenly Witt seemed to shrink into himself. He looked desperately tired, as if the prospect had tapped the source of his spirit in advance. He passed his hand over his lined forehead, streaked with dust and soot, over the pale, pale eye now as flat and colorless as a midwinter sky, over the broken nose that made two sharp changes of direction before coming to an end above his grimly drawn mouth.

He looked past the doctor to the horizon. It was ringed with mountainous gray clouds. Somewhere in the adjacent county it was raining, a cloudburst. He stared at the gauzy blue veil that hung from the thunderheads and trailed across the ground. When he spoke, his voice was pensive and heavy. "Why can't those people leave me alone? For the life of me I can't figure that one out. I'm getting old. I haven't had anything to do with any of them for the most part of my life. Why do they have to come around now, when I find it harder and harder to fight back? It's always been sort of a game between Roseanne and me, a needling game, like two fighting

167

pups that never draw blood. But, goddammit . . . now she's biting hard."

Koury wanted to put his hand on Witt's shoulder, but the old man looked so frail, so suddenly spent, that he held back, afraid even the gentle weight would bring him down.

Witt leaned against the porch railing for support. Breaking the silence, a mockingbird shrieked from a nearby tree and took wing. It flashed a dark ominous silhouette against the bright sky. Witt shuddered and followed it until it disappeared from sight.

Koury spoke at last. "What are you going to do?"

Witt's mind had been far away. He was thinking about the pyramid and how he wanted to live to see it finished. He was thinking about Noelia and what would become of her after he was gone. Koury's question brought him back.

"I'll fight them," he answered simply. "I've always been a brawler."

But he had to clasp his hands behind his back to stop the trembling. He wasn't at all sure, despite what he said, that he had the strength, or the time, to survive the test.

That night at supper Witt was subdued and thoughtful. Noelia's dark eyes watched anxiously as he picked at his food. He shoved it listlessly around the plate, lifting his fork halfway to his mouth, then pausing as if suddenly arrested by a crowding thought that made him forget what he was about to do. She tried futilely to reach him, calling, "Señor," across the table.

At last he pushed his plate away and took a sip of water. Noelia got up, disappeared through the kitchen door, and returned with the pills. Ritually Witt took them into his hand, pressed his palm against his mouth, and drained the glass. He remained at the table a few moments more. When he saw

168

that Noelia was not looking, he slipped his clasped hand beneath the table and dropped the two unswallowed pills soundlessly onto the carpet at his feet. He gave them a blind nudge with the toe of his boot and rolled them beneath the center pedestal so Noelia wouldn't find them. Then he scraped his chair back and stood up.

He had begun the experiment. He would give the pink pills an opportunity to do their work alone. He was afraid he was going to have to work fast.

Later Noelia joined him on the porch. The sun had set. Once again it was cool, a subtle mildness with breezes from the north that presaged winter. He felt her shiver as she snuggled in next to him.

"You ought to have a sweater, baby," he said softly. "Your arms are cold."

Noelia shook her head. "I'm warm next to you."

Witt looked at her curled up like a child beside him. He took her hands and rubbed the chill from her fingers.

She sat upright, now taking his hands in hers. "Señor, what's the matter?"

"Nothing to worry you, baby."

"Tell me, Señor. I can see it in your face."

Witt sighed. "It's my kinfolk. They've got their eyes on this place and are trying their damnedest to cheat me out of it." He explained to her about the hearing, slowly and quietly so as not to alarm her.

She listened intently. When he finished she squeezed his hands and said, "Don't worry. Everything will be okay. I'll go to the church and pray for us. I'll light a candle to the Lady of the Windmill."

Witt couldn't keep from smiling. He pressed her head close to his chest so she wouldn't see his lips. He didn't want her to think he was laughing at her.

169

CHAPTER SEVENTEEN

A young man in uniform had been standing at Katie's door for several minutes without a response to his persistent pressure on the doorbell. He knew the button was working. He could hear the bell ring on the other side of the closed door. And he knew there was someone at home, because he caught a movement in an upstairs window as he made his way up the walk. Like the children who watched from the wild bushes beneath swaying salt cedars, he sensed a chilling desolation about the place.

A white-bellied lizard had been clinging to the lintel above his head. Suddenly it blinked its bead-bright eyes and with a flick of its tail skittered headfirst down the flaking jamb, scattering dry leaves along the ground with a papery rustle.

He shivered and pressed the button again, hoping now that no one would answer. The house exuded the air of an untended graveyard. He was tempted to turn and run, to make his escape down the uneven walk that lay nearly buried by the encroaching, overgrown grass.

A muffled sound behind the door told him he had lingered too long. He stepped back, wanting to bolt but knowing that now he must stay.

Katie's voice came through the door. It was thin and unsteady. She said, "Wally?"

The young man took a breath and said, "Mrs. McIntosh?"

"Is that you, Wally?"

"It's Captain Dowland, ma'am," the young man answered leaning toward the closed door. He repeated his name and added, "I believe the Army wrote you about me . . . that I was coming."

There was no reply. During the long silence that followed, the young man hoped she had gone away, that once again he would have the chance to flee. But before he could make up his mind to turn and leave he heard the bolt slide back, scraping in its wooden track. Two haggard, cloudy eyes peered out of the dark opening. They studied him. He was tall and blond with a face so tanned it seemed to have no eyebrows. His uniform was freshly pressed but revealed by the horizontal crease at the knees that it had newly come from a suitcase. He had removed his service hat and held it between his elbow and waist. Bright ribbons made a rainbow-hued patch over his chest; silver captain's bars glinted on each shoulder.

"How do you do, ma'am?" he said.

Again Katie gave no answer. She stood in the half-opened door, looking at him, moving her lips silently, attempting to form words out of the cloudy thoughts that fluttered through her brain like black ashes in currents of rising heat. She passed her hands over her uncombed hair, trying to smooth it down at the sides. She gave up and fumbled with the belt of her kimono, that gaped open nearly to the waist.

Her half-nakedness embarrassed him. "Maybe I should come back later." He set his cap squarely on his head.

"Wait!" she said. She held out her hand to stop him. He could almost feel its trembling touch across the space that separated them. "No, don't leave! Come in."

171

Captain Dowland removed his cap once more and caught the screen door as Katie pushed it open. She led him through the dark foyer into the curtained living room's deeper gloom. The furniture was dull with dust. A waft of stale air brushed past their shoulders.

He would have preferred to remain standing, but Katie waved him onto the couch. He realized she was drunk. She swayed unsteadily on her feet, jamming her chin into her throat to hold back the rising swells of nausea. Whiskey stank through the house.

"Who are you?" she managed to say. Her voice was a strangled whisper.

"I was your son's commander. Wally was in my company." He paused. Only an unco-ordinated nod told him she heard. His uneasiness prodded him on. "The Army sent me . . . personally . . . because of the, uh, the incident." He couldn't bring himself to speak concretely of the coffin and the monkey.

Katie rocked on her heels. She struggled to bring the captain's vague outline into focus. "Wait a minute," she said. "Give me time. I'm trying . . . you see, I'm trying to follow you."

The captain kept silent and watched her sway. He was wondering what to do if she should suddenly start to fall.

She thrust out her hand and groped for the mantelpiece. Her outstretched fingers struck a framed photograph. He saw immediately that it was Wally. The dead boy's eyes swept the room as the picture skewed across the mantel. He held his breath, horrified. It crashed to the floor, strewing a swath of slivered glass along the carpet. He sprang from the couch, but Katie waved him back. "That's all right . . . that's all right. Don't bother. I'll get it." She stooped, nearly falling, and picked up the shattered frame. "I broke it. I smashed the glass."

"Please, let me help you," Captain Dowland said. He rose again.

"Leave it, leave it. You'll cut yourself," Katie mumbled. "I'll get a broom . . . later. I'll sweep it up." She motioned him back to the couch. "I'm always breaking things. Mirrors! God, I've broken so many mirrors I'm going to have to live to be a hundred just to . . . to get out from under all the bad luck I've got stored up."

Captain Dowland watched and listened. He was too horrified to speak.

She caressed the photograph. "This is my boy Wally."

The captain nodded. He was desperate to get his business over with.

"He hasn't come home from the war."

"Yes, ma'am, I know."

She looked up, her eyes sharp for the first time. "Where is he?"

Captain Dowland frowned. He was unprepared for that.

"Where is Wally? He's still alive, isn't he? I write him letters. They don't come back. Doesn't that prove he's still alive?"

Captain Dowland stood up. No one warned him she thought her son had survived. "I saw him die, ma'am."

Across the room Katie stood alone, holding the photograph against her breast. A tangle of blond hair drooped over her forehead, covering one eye. Captain Dowland could see the other one growing wet and filling with tears. A hoarse sob from deep inside her exploded from her lips.

"Mrs. McIntosh!"

She snapped her head back, tossing the hair out of her eye, blinking dry the tears. A wild fierceness came over her face. Captain Dowland stepped backward, afraid to approach her. "Ma'am, are you all right?"

She squared her big shoulders and stood tall. "Tell me! I'm strong as a rock. Tell me!" A new tear found its way out of

173

the corner of her eye and trickled over the curve of her cheek. She made no effort to brush it away.

"We were on a patrol," Captain Dowland said. He fought to control the trembling that shook through every word. "Clean-up operation . . . a routine maneuver. We'd been through the same thing lots of times before. There wasn't much to do. The area had been pretty well worked over before our turn came. We came upon some bodies, but it was so quiet we were sure if any of the enemy survived they must have gotten away already. Wally was off to the side along the left flank."

He paused, rubbing his temples, trying to get the sequence of events absolutely correct. "I had my eyes on him, you know, trying to look everywhere at once. One second he was there, walking along with the rest of us. He took another step and there was an explosion. It knocked us all down. Then . . . then all hell broke loose. Snipers laid into us, fire coming from all the trees. They got four of my men before we cleaned them out. When it was all over we buried those four. But Wally . . . ma'am, it was a mine! I hate to say it, but it's the truth: there was no use even looking for him. There wouldn't have been . . ."

He stopped. He couldn't tell her that a handkerchief could have covered Wally's remains. "It was quick. I swear to God he never knew it."

He shuddered and watched Katie. She had not moved since he began talking, and for a long time in the silence which followed she remained quite still, clutching the photograph to her body. Finally, a frown swept across her forehead, a transient fleeting cloud. She said, "But the letters . . . and the packages. I never got them back. You'd think that meant something."

"If it will set your mind at ease . . . we didn't leave him there alive. There never was any chance . . ."

174

She laid the photograph on the mantel and buried her face in her hands, breathing deeply into her palms. Captain Dowland watched wordlessly, wondering what was coming next, aching to leave the dark, morbid house and the miserable, disheveled woman whose son he had seen die.

At first he wasn't sure he had understood correctly; but she said it again and he heard her clearly: "Thanks . . . thanks." She was nodding her head, with her face still hidden in her hands. She kept repeating in a flat voice, "Thanks . . . thanks . . . thanks . . ."

He took this as a dismissal. He picked up his cap from the couch and tucked it under his arm. Katie paid him no attention. He moved tentatively toward the door. Once more he heard her say, "Thanks." She did not look up when he turned the doorknob.

He paused on the threshold. "All I can say is I'm sorry. I . . . uh, I don't know any more. The casket, well, it's just one of those things. In war everything is confusing."

Katie had dropped her hands. She was nodding silently, staring at the broken glass which glinted darkly across the carpet.

"I'm telling you the truth, ma'am. Things happened with no rhyme or reason. We hardly ever understood anything ourselves. I'm sorry . . . real, real sorry."

Katie nodded again without looking up.

She heard the door slam shut, then the quick clatter of the captain's heels as he fled across the porch and down the walk.

She jumped forward and tore through the door. She burst onto the porch in a frenzy.

"You lie!" she screamed. But the captain had disappeared. She stumbled against the railing and sagged to her knees, covering her swollen face with her hands. She was sobbing violently.

The children watched her heaving body curl into a knot. They kept silent as she rolled over onto her side. They listened to her sobs diminish. Then they looked at one another, wise looks of relief. "She's dead," the eldest said. His companions, two girls and a boy, nodded in wordless agreement. Still they waited, concealed in the overhanging branches, certain they were right, but cautiously waiting on the chance they might be wrong. Katie never moved. After a while they stole one by one out of their watching place and approached the porch.

The eldest brushed his black hair back out of his eyes and paused at the bottom of the steps. He studied the woman for any sign of life. She was lying on her side with her face covered. One leg was curled up beneath her, exposing her thigh's smooth white flesh. There was no sound.

The others waited until the eldest started up the steps. They followed him three abreast onto the porch and formed a circle around the prostrate figure. They stared at her for a long time, fascinated, as if they had found an odd and horrible fish cast dead upon a beach. Finally one of the girls said, "He got her. The ghost finally got her."

The others accepted this fact in silence.

Through the latticework of her fingers Katie stared up in wild confusion at the four solemn, somber faces above her. She had the impression she was lying in a coffin being lowered into the ground, the victim in a macabre ceremony overseen by a band of children. She saw their lips moving again and caught their statements' tattered ends as if their words were being whipped about by the rushing wind that blustered through her ears. She felt a deathly coldness making icy cylinders of her fingers and her toes. She lay perfectly still

176

with no wish for breath, no urge to blink away the burning air that dried the stinging tears from the surface of her eyes. Perhaps this is what Witt meant when he spoke of Death as something real, as something which touched you and came for you. The thought ripped across her brain like a bramble thorn.

Her body had almost ceased to function. She had not drawn a breath for some time. Darkness coiled into enclosing circles around her eyes, as if she were sinking into a deep well. At the top, staring down at her, far, far away, were the four children. Were they mourning her? Were they lowering her into this chasm? Was this death?

Through the roaring wind which churned wildly up the deepening shaft, she thought she heard one say, "She's dead."

And for a moment she imagined she was.

But then the eldest bent over the hole's dark edge and extended his arm. It seemed to her an impossible distance between them. Surely there was no way the child's arm could reach her! But down it came, stretching longer and longer until her heart gave a flutter. She felt the blood surge suddenly warm through her limbs. She felt her throat retching for air. She thought, "He's reaching for me! He's trying to pull me out of this hole!"

In a last desperate attempt to save herself, she threw up her arms and grabbed his hand. She grasped it in both of hers. The boy yanked back in blind fear, horrified. The roaring wind that deafened her ears during her miraculous ascent smothered the terrified cries of the other children, howling at the sight of her corpse coming back to life. The boy's face twisted as if he had taken hold of a writhing snake. He wrenched his hand free and plunged after his companions scattering from the house.

Released suddenly from his grip, Katie felt herself tottering.

177

She screamed, frightened that once again she would hurtle back into the pit's howling darkness. But she had seen it, had fallen nearly to its bottom, had witnessed the living circle of light at its top growing small. She flailed her arms in wild desperation. She fought to save her life. Her fingertips crashed against the railing. She grabbed the peeling slats and hauled herself forward away from the pit. She locked her arms around them until the swirling, shrieking wind died down.

She knew she had escaped. She knew she had cheated something that had tried to claim her. She raised her head and looked into the house. The formless terror was still there, waiting for her inside, a mute, certain patience that could reclaim her again.

She stood before the door knowing that to re-enter, to dwell in there again, would be to let its dark, smothering shroud wrap its folds around her and carry her back down . . . deeper this time, farther and farther into the pit until she struck bottom.

She grew steady on her feet, sobered by this realization. Then, not without pain, with the feeling of leaving behind a loved one who had grown evil, too poisonous to live with, she descended the porch steps into the open air.

Father Anselmo was breaking in a new organist.

"Now, Gloria," he said to the tense young girl on the bench before the console, "if you keep your eyes on this light bulb, we'll have no more embarrassing mistakes at tomorrow's Mass like we suffered last Sunday: no more Credos during the Gospel, no Sanctus during the Offertory, and no one will have to remain after church for you to finish the Agnus Dei."

Gloria, still mortified by the previous week's humiliation, gnawed nervously at her fingernails and watched as Father Anselmo tightened a light bulb into the socket he had just

178

attached to the top of the church organ. With a flush of pride at his own inventiveness, the priest stepped back to admire the gadget he had contrived.

"Here's how it will work," he explained to Gloria. "I've installed a button on the altar. When I press it, the light will glow. That's your signal to begin playing. It's very simple. You have only to watch the bulb. Do you understand?"

"Yes, Father," Gloria mumbled through her fingers.

"Now, all that remains is to connect the button with the light." He pitched a coil of wire over the choir loft into the empty nave below. "It shouldn't take more than a few minutes; then we'll test it."

"What shall I play?" Gloria asked, eager to get everything right.

"Anything! I don't want a whole concert, though. Just strike a chord to let me know if the light has turned on. And quit chewing your fingers or you'll bleed on the organ." As he descended the stairs he couldn't resist calling back cattily: "While you're waiting, you might have a few sorely needed words with St. Cecilia."

Gloria whizzed through a quick prayer. She then pulled out all the stops, stepped down hard on the swell pedal, and limbered up her knuckles. Her eyes zeroed in on the light bulb, alert for her cue.

Below, Father Anselmo retrieved the coil of wire. He unreeled it down the side aisle, threaded it through the altar rail, and stretched it taut across the sanctuary floor. Then he carried it out of sight behind the green velvet arras that backed the altar. Through a parting in the heavy curtain bristled a stiff strand of wire, which was attached at its other end to the button on the altar. Father Anselmo ascended his spindly stepladder, fished in his pocket for his penknife, and began stripping the wires of their insulation.

At that moment Noelia arrived at San Pablo's to offer her prayer to the Lady of the Windmill. She paused for an instant to cover her head with her mantilla, then slipped inside through the front door.

She crossed herself with holy water and stood uncertainly in the wide aisle, trying to decide which saint to pray before. All the way into town she had fretted over the problem, and now she cast a warily appraising eye over the various statues ensconced on painted plaster-cloud pedestals. She rejected St. Theresa out of hand, considering her overworked because a host of smoky votive lights already flickered at her sandaled feet. Blessed Martin de Porres couldn't be relied on, not being finally canonized. Nor was she sold on Gregory the Wonderworker, whose name sounded promising but about whom she knew little. Since she had lost nothing she quickly disregarded St. Anthony, and St. Rose of Lima had failed her in the past.

She sighed and began to consider the procession of saints huddled in shallow niches along the other wall.

Behind the velvet arras, Father Anselmo worked with leisurely thoroughness. Once the last clinging shred of insulation was stripped from the copper wires, he twisted the two ends together and wrested from his back pocket a roll of black friction tape. Warmed by satisfaction with his handiwork, he began to hum *O Salutaris*.

The hymn's droning strains wafted through the nave, alerting Noelia. Her skin crawled with a sudden prickling as if someone had stealthily blown in her ear.

Surely another vision is coming, she thought. Her pulse quickened as the humming grew louder. She glanced about wide-eyed until she located its source: the music was emanating from the altar itself!

She let herself be drawn forward up the aisle. Without

180

hesitation she climbed over the communion rail, crossed the sanctuary carpet, and ascended the three steps until she found herself at the altar. Eager to miss nothing she blinked back tears that threatened to cloud her fluttering eyes.

The melody ended with the briefest silence, only to begin again with greater vigor and an almost jiglike tempo, a deep joyful baritone resonating out of thin air from above the tabernacle.

Surely an angel's voice, Noelia thought with mounting fervor. The music enveloped her and lured her on. With quick, soundless gasps she hauled herself onto the altar until she was kneeling directly before the gleaming tabernacle. She raised her eyes to the foot of the cross above her head and steeled herself for the vision. At last, when she was prepared, she whispered breathlessly: *"Madre de Dios! Estoy lista!"*

The deep humming ceased in mid-note. The curtain behind the crucifix began to billow, sending Noelia into a near swoon. Her eyes roved wildly in their sockets.

Suddenly the curtain parted. Father Anselmo's pale face, disembodied by the darkness beyond, appeared eye to rolling eye with Noelia's. He blinked in disbelief. His mouth sagged. Noelia cringed in confusion.

"Sacrilege!" Father Anselmo gasped, his trembling body tottering dangerously on the shaky ladder. "Fiend! What are you doing kneeling on my altar?"

Noelia shrank away from him, shuffling sideways. As she scuttled across the altar her knee came down heavily on the small button.

In the choir loft the light bulb flashed brightly. Gloria's poised fingers plummeted onto the keys, raising a chord that rocked the church. The trumpeting echo flew among the rafters. Noelia shrieked with fear and went ashen.

"Devil!" Father Anselmo hissed.

"Where?" Noelia cried. She swung around in panic just as Gloria's dark figure rose like a specter from behind the organ.

Noelia opened her mouth wide and screamed.

Father Anselmo felt the ladder lurch ominously beneath him. He grabbed for the curtain, jostling its heavy folds against the altar's six golden candlesticks, setting them rocking on their bases.

Noelia turned around and screamed again, convinced the candlesticks' wild dance was a stunt of the devil.

As abruptly as it had appeared, Father Anselmo's stricken face vanished from view. From behind the curtain came a dull thud, followed by a hoarse moan.

The candlesticks continued their dervish dance, whirling closer and closer to the altar's edge. Then one by one, with tantalizing precision, they somersaulted with a deafening clatter to the floor.

Noelia sprang from the altar and cleared the communion rail with a running leap. She hurtled down the aisle, wailing shrilly for the Virgin to save her.

The shock of the heavy door slamming behind her was too much for the old crucifix. The tortured figurine slipped its bonds of rusty wire and plummeted in a graceful swan dive to the altar below.

From his porch Witt observed a suspended slab of granite, cradled in cables, float slowly through the air. Its shadow inched along the ground and slid up the six completed tiers of solid stone that now rose nearly thirty feet above the plain's flat floor. The crane's whine dropped abruptly as its driver halted the swinging arm and began lowering the slab. There was a quick shout, another change in pitch, and suddenly the stone was in place—the start of another level.

In the rays of the afternoon sun the sloping west wall

182

burned pink like glowing flesh. The wall facing him, in shadow, was blood dark. The stunted structure rearing up before him looked *already* ancient, the eroded remains of a once soaring monument set afire again and again by countless sunrises and sunsets, baked into nature's colors by an era of blazing arcs across the sky, gnawed at and worn away by a succession of days, adding up to centuries, that dawned dark with rain and wild with wind until its lofty apex was ground to dust that scattered itself particle by particle among the surrounding sands. Time—using itself as its final weapon! And yet the thing still stood!

Witt's mind leaped forward ten thousand years. It saw the pyramid as perhaps it would be then, retreating from its turn among the swimming clouds in the burning blue-white sky, returning its stony mantle to the earth from which it had sprung. Yet still it stood, marking time, marking place. He felt a thrill in his old body. He knew he would be satisfied.

The ringing of the phone . . . persistent, urgent; it dragged him away from the railing and into the house. His mind lingered behind with the pyramid, withstanding time, overleaping death.

He said hello.

It was Roseanne.

Her voice pulled the breath from his body. She stood before him able to do what neither the sun, nor the wind, nor the rain . . . not even time . . . would achieve. She could destroy him. She could pull his pyramid to the ground even before it stood full height. She could erase with fields of grass the scar it would leave behind.

Witt heard her speaking, slowly and clearly as if explaining to a child. There was a hollowness to her voice, and he realized, even before he understood what she was talking

183

about, that someone else was on the line, a third party eavesdropping on an extension, listening silently to what passed between them. Roseanne was being thorough. She had a witness.

She quit talking. There was a long pause, a thin, drawn-out silence, a tautly pulled string scratched by random crackles of static resonating with low, regular breathing from someone else besides the two of them.

Roseanne spoke again. "You didn't understand what I was saying, did you, Witt?" Her voice carried a guarded archness, a verbal trick—the deliberate emphasis one uses with a cohort to solicit his corroboration in a sudden lie. But Roseanne had twisted the trick one further turn. She pulled at Witt to back her up before her accomplice.

Witt felt the tug. He knew there was something wrong, but he stumbled, acting faster than he thought. "No . . . what?" He was still struggling for breath.

Roseanne let his mumbled question germinate in the silence, a pointed silence which charged the words with confusion. The breathing from the third telephone interrupted its own rhythm as if to emphasize that the point had been noted. Then Roseanne went on:

"I said there's no cause to get excited or worried. We're concerned about you, Witt. That's all. Concerned about your health. That's why we want you to go with Seyton and Floyd to see a doctor in San Antonio."

"Give it up, Roseanne. I've had enough of this goddamn game."

Another long silence; another interruption in the regular breathing.

"Now, Witt . . ." she began.

"There's nothing wrong with me."

"We want to be sure."

"You want to lock me up, that's what you're working at."

184

"Now, who said anything about locking you up? The very idea." There was almost a tinkle of a laugh to her voice, as if the thought were startling, even shocking. She began again, speaking slowly and deliberately, as if her words were being measured and recorded. "We want you to see the doctor, willingly, of your own accord."

"To hell with you! And the others! You think I don't know exactly what you're up to?"

Roseanne broke in. "I'm sorry, Witt. I can't talk to you when you don't make sense. You're hard to understand when you say funny things like that." She paused. There was a muffled sound, a brief deadening of the wire, as her hand clapped over the mouthpiece and moved away again. "Witt, I'm going to go now. I'll call you back later, when you're thinking more clearly, and we can talk sense."

"I know what kind of sense you're talking about!" he shouted; but he was holding a dead phone. Roseanne had hung up.

He slammed the receiver down, knocking the telephone to the floor, wanting to rip it out of the wall, but he was too tired, too drained of energy to do more than slump into the nearest chair and throw his head back for deep swallows of air. His mind buzzed and sputtered like a generator running wild, a whirring catherine wheel throwing off white sparks that blossomed like star shells against the dome of his skull. He called aloud for Noelia, for in the center of every exploding star he could see her face, her wide loving eyes like polished agate, the warm skin, the soft full lips, smiling, showing her teeth. *"Noelia!"* he cried again, frightened that he was dying.

Roseanne's demeanor was businesslike. She waited for Seyton to join her from the bedroom where he had been listening on the extension. When he entered the den she

185

turned her palms upward and raised her eyebrows, as if to say, "What could be simpler?"

Seyton answered her with a quick nod.

She rose. "Well, now it's up to you. I've tried to get him to see a doctor under his own steam and you're my witness. I swan, I never heard more bad talk in all my life." Her voice trailed off as she waited for Seyton's confirmation.

He nodded again.

"So what's the next step?" she asked, tossing him his signal. Why did *she* always have to call the play?

"There's nothing left but to get a court order," Seyton said, falling into line. "If he won't enter a hospital on his own, we'll have to force him there." He looked up to see if this met with her approval.

Roseanne fired up a cigarette and smiled. "Well, *that's* a little matter between you and Smokey."

When Noelia returned from San Pablo's she found Witt still in the chair. He opened his eye. She was kneeling before him, her head still scarfed in the mantilla. Her eyes searched his face. He grabbed her as if afraid she was going to leave him. When she saw him move and felt his arms around her she burst into tears. "Oh, Señor, Señor, what happened to you?"

Witt didn't know. He thought he was having another stroke. But he could move. He didn't feel sick. "I'm okay," he said hoarsely, proving to himself he could speak. He moved his legs. He would be able to stand too. "I must have fallen asleep," he said. "A bad dream, I guess, a nightmare."

He held her close. For a moment he wondered if the telephone call from Roseanne had been a dream also, but he saw the telephone overturned on the floor and knew it had been real.

186

He pulled the mantilla from her head and stroked her long black hair, letting it fall like silk through his fingers. It tumbled over her shoulders and spilled across his chest. He fanned it out until it glistened like spun sugar. Then he gathered it together again into a thick coil and let it overflow his palms. Noelia closed her eyes and tucked her head beneath his chin.

"Where have you been, baby?" he murmured, too tired to speak above a whisper. Her mantilla lay draped over the chair, where he had dropped it.

Noelia's fingers crept like silent soldiers across the upholstery, encircled the lacy mantilla, and began stuffing it beneath the cushion. She kept her face between his and the scarf as she worked to tuck it out of sight. "I've been in town to see Tia Cecilia."

Witt snared the tail end of the mantilla before it disappeared beneath the cushion. He tugged until it slipped from her fingers and fell between them. He caught the shadow of a mischievous smile tracing the corners of her lips.

Neither spoke for a moment. He could see Noelia's mind racing for an explanation that he would buy. Then he smiled, too tired not to. Noelia broke into a bright, nervous laugh.

"Oh, Señor! Why don't you believe me?"

Witt teased the mantilla with his forefinger. "Because you don't wear this thing just to go see Tia Cecilia."

Noelia thought for a moment, then draped the mantilla over her face, obscuring her features. The game she was going to play would work better if he couldn't see her eyes. "You be the priest, and I will tell you my confession. Turn your head sideways . . . like that. The priest shouldn't look."

Witt complied with the pressure of her fingers on his cheek and stared off at the blank wall.

"*Bueno*," Noelia began. "I went to San Pablo's to talk to the Lady."

"What lady?" Witt turned and looked at her.

She scolded him with an upright finger and averted his head again. "No fair looking."

He obeyed.

"I went to pray to my Lady . . . the Lady of the Windmill. I told her about your family and what they want to do to you. I asked her to stop them."

She paused.

"Is that all?"

"Yes. No more." She crossed her heart.

He pulled the mantilla away from her face, unmasking her. "Are you sure?"

She lowered her eyelids. He watched her carefully. "Noelia . . . ?" His voice was deeply suspicious, rising at the end as one would threaten a child stubbornly persisting in an outrageous fib.

He saw her shrug at last. She took a long breath. He waited.

"Just like I said. I went to talk to the Lady. I told her all about you and your trouble, and . . . and oh! the Lady was angry. Very angry!"

Witt pulled his head back and stared at her. "Oh, she was? Now, how do you know that?"

"She gave me a sign."

"A sign?"

Noelia nodded excitedly, carried away. Her face glowed. As she talked she raised her eyes to the ceiling as if it had suddenly opened up for her to the blue sky beyond. "She made a miracle, right there in the church. You see, the devil came to stop me from praying. This made the Lady so mad because it's the devil who's causing your family to do bad

188

things to you. The Lady wanted to drive him away. She knocked the candlesticks off the altar. She threw them on the floor and told me to get out of the church quick . . . before the devil could get me."

"And . . ." Witt urged.

Noelia shrugged again. "And that's all. But that means she's going to help."

Witt looked disappointed that there was no more. Noelia decided to add the final touch. "Father Anselmo was there. He saw the devil. I heard him yell at him."

She looked at Witt. He was silent for a moment as he considered her story. Finally, in a gesture between a nod and a shrug, he said, "One thing, baby, you sure as fire see the damnedest sights!"

Noelia acknowledged this with sublime gravity and wove her fingers through Witt's old, gnarled hands.

CHAPTER EIGHTEEN

With a frighteningly close election breathing down his neck, Judge Smokey Matthews had gotten cold feet. "Goddammit, Seyton, I don't like the smell of it. It ain't so cut and dried like it seemed before."

He rummaged through his desk's top drawer and pulled out the latest issue of *Life*. He didn't have to ask if Seyton had seen it. Everyone in Landry had. He dropped the magazine on top of the cluttered desk and flipped to a dog-eared page.

A PYRAMID RISES ABOVE THE TEXAS PLAIN, ran the caption above the enormous photograph of the pyramid, black beams sharply outlined against a cloudless sunset. Opposite was Witt's picture. Beneath the Stetson's curled brim his eye glowered suspiciously into the camera. The type below read: "Eccentric Millionaire Becomes Modern Cheops."

Seyton averted his eyes. There were other pictures and other captions, but he didn't want to be reminded. Smokey was relentless. He put on his glasses and read aloud in his best voice from the bench: "Landry's long-time mayor, A. B. 'Dutch' Holland is pleased with his town's newfound notoriety. 'This had put us on the map. Our nickname's always been the Sweet Heart of South Texas. Now we have a pyramid to mark the spot.' At right, behind his desk at Landry's only bank, Vice-President Albert Pugh sees a shot in the arm for the town's economy. 'We've got the welcome mat out for the tourists. They'll want food and someplace to sleep. We aim to accommodate them. I think it means a new prosperity for Landry.' "

Smokey would have droned on through another half-dozen enthusiastic comments, but Seyton threw up his hands and stopped the recitation. "I already read it, Smokey. I know everything it says."

Smokey peered over his glasses. "Do you get the point I'm trying to make?"

Seyton obstinately refused to answer. He understood all too well. Public reaction had surprised and disconcerted both of them. Instead of thinking Witt crazy, people were cheering him as a hero who had given Landry something to be proud of. There was no doubt about it: signing a court order to put Witt away and halt work on the pyramid would do wonders for Smokey's political opponent.

Seyton ventured a look at him. Smokey's pointed stare told him to forget the action. He groped for something to say. "They called him eccentric! Did you see that? *Life* magazine came right out and said Witt was eccentric. Let me see that magazine and I'll show you where. . . ."

"Hell, Seyton," Smokey growled, snatching the magazine out of reach. "*Life* magazine calls lots of people eccentric. That don't mean they're insane."

Seyton slumped unhappily in his chair.

Smokey clasped his hands primly together across his belly and began to pontificate. "Your timing's all off. Everybody's worked up about this pyramid right now, dreaming of getting rich quick when the tourists start pouring in. They're even talking about changing the name of the football team to the

191

Pharaohs!"—a bit of news he invented on the spot. "You'd just rile the hell out of a lot of folks if you go messing around with Witt. My advice is to hold your fire. Let all the commotion simmer down. You know what I mean?"

Seyton knew exactly. Smokey was worried about the election. With the race so tight he wasn't in the mood for risks. But Seyton knew too that Roseanne and Possom's ship was sinking fast. Their next payment was due and they had nothing.

He wiped away the sweat tickling his pink upper lip. "Believe me, Smokey, I appreciate your position, but I got trouble and I got to work fast."

Smokey's eyes grew beady. "You know your business, Seyton, but I can't see my way clear to help you. If you press the hearing, I'm going to have to disqualify myself."

Seyton was on his feet fuming. "You can't do that!"

"Just watch." Smokey pretended to find something interesting in the *Life* article.

Seyton wanted to ram the magazine down his throat, but struggled to control himself. His knuckles went white as he gripped the desk. Smokey was the only judge in his pocket and he couldn't let him go. When at last he managed to speak, he was hoarse and gravel-voiced. "You can't skip out on me like that, Smokey. It just ain't that easy. I got the goods on you, so many hair-raising tales that if I let them out even you wouldn't be caught dead voting for yourself."

Smokey banged both fists on his desk. "Hold it! Before you go threatening blackmail, just remember, I got a story or two on you. . . ."

"I reckon you do," Seyton said smoothly, "but there's one big difference—I ain't the one who's running for election." He smiled with new confidence.

192

Smokey grabbed the copy of *Life* to throw at him, but Seyton ducked his fuzzy pink head and slipped out the door.

Witt was still wide awake when the telephone rang at midnight. He left his bed and padded barefoot down the dark hall to the kitchen and picked up the receiver.

"Hello?"

"Witt Tyler? Is that you?"

The caller was trying to disguise his voice, but Witt knew in an instant it was Smokey Matthews.

The judge went on, speaking through a folded handkerchief, innocently confident the trick was working. "You don't know who this is, but I've got something mighty important to tell you."

Witt was mystified but he played along. "What is it, stranger?"

"I happen to know that certain parties in town have it in mind to get you declared *non compos mentis.*"

The old anger boiled up in Witt. He caught himself from revealing that he already knew. The call intrigued him. He wanted to know what Smokey was up to. "You don't say? Who would be wanting to do that to me?"

Smokey ignored the question. He was going to say only as much as necessary, nothing more. "I also happen to know that you and Hector Sanchez's daughter haven't been properly married, leastwise according to state law, and I'm including common law union in this."

Witt's jaw tightened. He wanted to tell Smokey he was stepping out of bounds. What passed between him and Noelia was none of the judge's business. But Smokey rushed on. "So, as things stand, these certain parties have got the law behind them. They can get their hands on you."

There was a dramatic pause, as if the judge expected Witt to relieve him from continuing by filling in the rest. Witt

193

held his silence and waited. At last Smokey conceded and went on. Witt could hear him sighing with every word.

"Don't you see, man? If you get yourself married to this . . . this lady, and I mean married legal-like, she would automatically become your next-of-kin. Then nobody else, including these certain parties, could raise a case against you."

Witt nodded dumbly. There was the solution to the problem that had kept him lying awake half the night.

"You understand what I'm saying?" Nervous exasperation caused Smokey to forget his disguise. His voice boomed across strong and clear.

"I follow you," Witt said. "How long do I have?"

Smokey hesitated, then said, "No time to fool around. Get your blood test tomorrow. You gotta hurry, man. The goddamn waiting period is three days."

"I'll have that long then?"

"I'll do my best to hold things back."

"Why are you telling me all this?"

There was instant silence on Smokey's part. Then he said, "Lordie, don't ask. Just do what I say."

The phone clicked dead.

After a while Witt got up from the kitchen stool and stood at the window. He watched the cranes swing through the night air in the floodlit glare. He heard the grinding gears from across the flat land. For an instant the cranes hesitated in their dreamlike dance as if there had been a break in the music. Then they began their fluid swing in the opposite direction until their arms hovered over the storage pile of granite slabs. There was a sharp blast from a whistle and the ground crew scrambled to attach another heavy block to the dangling cables; on and on, over and over again, the cranes performed their carefully choreographed gyrations while Witt watched mesmerized from the window. The stone row

194

turned the corner and continued its slow, deliberate march down the far, steeply canted side.

He left the kitchen and moved to the porch, alternatively watching and dozing in his old wooden chair as the work progressed. The air was cool and fresh. A flight of whitewing cooed above the engines' steady drone. The sky lightened perceptibly above the glow around the pyramid. The flat land out as far as the horizon, which only moments before had been but a darker stain below the black night, took on a wash of silvery blue. The gulf clouds hung gray and woolly off to the east, their mounded tops catching the first prelight of dawn shining like bright castles on the crests of rolling blue mountains.

Yellow squares appeared along the sides of the workers' barracks as the morning crew arose and snapped on lights to wash and dress for the new shift. Pale smoke rose from the half-dozen chimneys protruding through the tin roofs of the kitchen shacks. Witt thought he smelled the odor of frying bacon. At last the upper crescent of the sun's disk slipped above the horizon. It drenched the land, the scrubby trees, the wooden barracks, and the pyramid's granite sides with a mist of morning light.

Witt stirred. He was stiff and cold from having passed the night in the hard chair on the porch, but his mind was sharp and active, ready to go, ready to act, as if by watching the walls of his pyramid climbing another tier in height he had recharged his soul with an untapped pool of energy.

He stood up. His joints crackled as he stretched his long arms and legs. He pushed through the kitchen door and reached for the telephone.

Witt let it ring for a long time. He glanced at the clock on the wall and decided that because of the early hour Father Anselmo would still be sleeping.

In fact, Father Anselmo had risen well before dawn. At the moment the telephone began ringing in his office he was again perched precariously on the top rung of his ladder, hanging the mended crucifix in place above the altar. He was in a hurry. He had to complete the job before the first arrivals for early Mass. He ignored the ringing and attached the crucifix to its rusty hooks. He let go, holding his breath until he was sure the wire and paste would hold. Only then did he descend the ladder and go for the phone.

"*Quién habla?*" he asked.

"Witt Tyler, Padre." He heard Father Anselmo's sharp intake of air. The priest said nothing; so Witt went on. "Do you know me?"

"*Sí sí,*" Father Anselmo gasped. "The . . . the friend of . . . of . . ." He could not bring himself to say her name.

Witt attributed his vagueness and halting, breathless speech to a still drowsy mind snatched from sleep. "Padre, I'm sorry I woke you up. I know it's early, but I don't have a lot of time."

With a quick sign of the cross Father Anselmo fired off a prayer to St. Theresa. "Save me from that crazy girl! No more visions! No more miracles! No more letters from the bishop!" The prayer took only a second; then he listened to what Witt was saying.

"You see, Padre, I want to get married. Me and Noelia. I know I'm giving you short notice, but . . ."

Wet, warm tears clouded Father Anselmo's eyes. He was thanking St. Theresa with a quivering smile: "You never fail me. Ah! With what speed you fly to my aid!"

"Well, Padre? Can it be arranged?"

"*Sí, señor, sí, sí!* No problem at all. It's just what I would have suggested. Whenever you want, immediately . . . I understand, right away!"

Witt woke Noelia and drove her to the hospital for the blood test. As they were leaving, he collared Dr. Koury in the corridor outside the lab.

"We're going to make it legal," he said, showing the red mark on his arm where the technician had drawn blood.

Koury's eyebrows lifted sharply. "You mean . . ."

Witt gave him a wink. "Oh, we went through some hocus-pocus, but this time we're doing it up right, going to San Pablo's to get the good words said over our heads." He leaned close to Koury and whispered in his ear. "Keep it under your hat, Doc. This is going to knock the props out from under Roseanne."

Koury grinned. "I'll never tell. It serves her right."

"Got some time to spare? I'd like to ask you something."

Koury looked at his watch. "I have just about one minute."

"That's about all the longer it will take." He motioned for Noelia to stay behind and drew Koury aside. "Doc, are you sure those pills are going to do the job?"

"Which pills?"

"You know . . . those potency pills." He looked over his shoulder at Noelia. "I would have thought by now we would have seen some evidence."

"Are you doing your part?" Koury asked.

"It's damn near killing me!" He was shaking his head earnestly.

Koury laughed in spite of himself. "Maybe you're trying too hard."

"Well, I don't know. I've been doing some thinking lately. Maybe it's not me that's holding up the show after all." He jabbed his thumb in Noelia's direction. "I mean, do you suppose she could use a pill or two?"

From the looks of her, Koury doubted it. "I tell you what,"

197

he said. "Bring her to see me. Call the nurse and set up an appointment for a checkup."

Witt's eye brightened. He broke into a smile. "Good idea, Doc. It would ease my mind."

From down the hall a nurse stepped out of a doorway and beckoned. Koury nodded at her and stepped away. "Just call my office, Witt. We'll try to find what's holding things up."

"Thanks a million, Doc. I'll be mighty obliged. It means a lot to me."

Koury smiled. "I'm sure it does."

Witt watched him hurry down the hall. He returned to Noelia's side and they left the hospital. They drove leisurely back to the ranch to pass the three-day waiting period.

It had consumed almost every ounce of Smokey's courage to telephone Witt and show him the way past Roseanne and Seyton. If events didn't work out exactly on schedule, he was certain he would be crushed in the squeeze. There wasn't much choice—Seyton's blackmail or the town's anger. Either road meant losing the election.

But if he could hold off issuing the court order until Witt was married, then he could dance away free. Seyton couldn't blame him for something he knew nothing about.

So Smokey delayed.

He left town and took his wife to Mexico. He left Clara, his secretary, to deal with Seyton. When Seyton called again at the courthouse to prod Smokey on, Clara put on her straight face and told him the judge had driven his wife to Houston. "It's just a quick little trip. Ida has to see a specialist. He'll be back in no time, don't you worry."

But Seyton fretted nervously. "Mighty sudden departure, it seems to me."

198

Clara fended him off with a smile. "He'll be sitting right there behind his desk tomorrow ready to talk. You mark my word."

Seyton went away grumbling. When he returned the next day and discovered that Smokey was still away he began to shout. "I think you two are cooking something up. It sure seems funny that all of a sudden . . ."

Clara shut him up. "He just called." The lie rolled from her tongue with a brightness that soothed Seyton. "He's beside himself he didn't make it back like he promised. It's Ida, you know. . . ." She lowered her voice, startling Seyton with a sudden, mournful look. "Poor thing, she's been feeling down in the mouth for the longest time. The doctors must've found something."

Seyton was distracted. "You mean . . . ?"

"Oh, I'm sure it's just a little upset and she'll turn out good as new." She gave Seyton a long, knowing look that told him she expected the worst.

Seyton shook his head sadly, "Poor Ida. I've known her all my life."

"Sweetest lady in town," Clara commiserated.

He was so taken by the idea that Ida Matthews had one foot in the grave he nearly forgot to ask when Smokey would be back.

"He told me on the phone he'd be in tomorrow at the latest. He said for you not to worry one little bit. He knows you're in a hurry and he'll be here if he's got to walk all the way from Houston."

Seyton sighed, somewhat relieved. He dreaded telling Roseanne.

That night Smokey and Ida slipped back into town, tanned brown from three days in the Mexican sun sipping tequila sours poolside at their Monterrey hotel. They hadn't had

199

such fun in ages. They could have lingered there a month. But Smokey couldn't postpone the meeting any longer. He tossed and turned all night. If Witt had taken advantage of the delay, he should be able to pick up the results of the blood test the next morning. Then he could take out the marriage license and make his march up the aisle. Smokey would not allow himself to think of the consequences if this tack was unsuccessful.

CHAPTER NINETEEN

Witt was up before dawn, keeping to schedule. For the first time in ages he pulled his dark blue gabardine out of the closet. He brushed it down, shook the pockets free of crumbled mothballs, and hung it in the window to air while he bathed in Noelia's pink marble tub. Then he dressed.

He had asked Colbert to be his best man. He found him hunched over the kitchen table with a cup of coffee. Colbert looked up as he entered. "Jesus Christ! That's some fancy tie you're wearing!"

"I feel just like a dude, all got up like this," Witt said. He looked down at the tie he had knotted with care. It was flaming red silk a handspan wide. Emblazoned in its center, so it would show between his coat lapels, was a huge hand-painted western saddle studded with fourteen-carat gold brads. He stuck out his chest to give Colbert a better look. The architect half scowled beneath his bushy eyebrows and shook his head in wonder.

Witt helped himself to coffee and leaned against the drain-board. "I want you to drive in to Landry ahead of us and give Katie McIntosh a lift to the church. She's moved out of her house. You'll find her waiting at the hotel. Noelia and I will be along shortly. We got to pick up the license first."

Colbert nodded, drained his cup, and banged through the back door jingling his car keys.

Witt was left alone in the silent house. Noelia had spent the night in her mother's trailer. He glanced anxiously at the clock and sat down at the table to sip his coffee. Minnie came sniffing at the back door, attracted by Colbert's departure. Witt called out to her, but she gave him a gaping, lazy yawn and padded gingerly on stiff legs to a spot of shade beneath the bougainvillaea arch.

Witt finished his coffee and reached behind him for the pot. Suddenly he heard Noelia's footsteps on the porch. He jumped up, surprised and thrilled by the urgent thumping in his chest. He threw open the door and she stood before him.

She peeked up from beneath mounds of fine white lace veiling her head. Her eyes blazed brightly. Her hair hung in two shining braids almost to her waist. Golden hoops dangled from her earlobes and flashed in the morning sunlight. Her face was dusted pale with white powder. Her lips, shyly parted as if they dared not smile yet ached to, were brushed with pink. She gathered up the skirt of her wedding dress and fanned it out for him, unfolding the bunches of stiff, snowy organdy that enveloped her like a rustling froth.

He threw out his arms and she came to him.

"Oh, Baby!" he cried. "You look like a queen!"

From the trailer doorway Carmen watched intently. She and Noelia had been up since five at work on their artistry. When she saw Witt's face as he took Noelia into his arms and drew her close, she smiled with satisfaction. She knew they had pleased *el Señor*.

Witt and Noelia boarded the Rolls-Royce for the ride to

202

town. Hector, Carmen, and the five children, moving heedfully in their Sunday finery, piled into the old pickup.

At the same moment, Roseanne was tapping her foot impatiently at her kitchen door. "You're slow as molasses, Possom! It won't surprise me if you're late for your own funeral."

Possom appeared from the hallway, tugging on his coat. "I still don't see why you're so fired up to drag me along."

"Because it doesn't look right for a woman to go to the courthouse on business without her husband. People are liable to think I'm there for a divorce." She gave him a pointed look. "Now shake a leg. If I know Seyton, he's about to have a hissy waiting on us."

So they set off, bound for the courthouse to get Smokey Matthews' signature on the court order to force Witt into a psychiatric exam, just as Witt and Noelia crossed the city limits, heading for the same destination to pick up their marriage license.

Roseanne was right. Seyton was pacing the floor and swearing, not because Roseanne and Possom were late, but because Smokey was.

"Helluva way to run a railroad!" he stormed at Clara.

She finished filling a thermos jug with coffee and slipped it into the judge's desk. "I reckon he's pretty pooped out," she said. "He didn't get in till late last night . . . with poor Ida." She laid the last words out before him like cards of doom.

Seyton clamped his lips shut and suffered in silence out of respect for Ida's tragic ailment.

In reality, Smokey was lying low in the adjoining office, stalling for a little more time. He had been camped there for over an hour, watching anxiously for Witt's car. Instead, he had seen Seyton arriving bright and early. Now he spotted Roseanne's Cadillac nosing around the corner in a cloud of yellow dust. It wallowed to a halt at the curb and her door flew open. She was halfway up the walk almost at a run before Possom could clamber out.

Smokey grimaced at her shrill curse as she burst into his office and was told he wasn't there. He half rose, shining with nervous perspiration. He couldn't put off his appearance much longer. A dark shadow crossed the corner of his eye. He dropped back in his seat and looked out the window. The gleaming Rolls-Royce was sailing up the street like a Spanish galleon. It heeled into the curb and dropped anchor.

"Thank the Lord!" Smokey sighed. He pulled a fat cigar from his shirt pocket, bit through the tip, and rolled it leisurely over his tongue. As Noelia and Witt stepped from the car he craned forward. He followed their arm-in-arm procession up the walk, wishing they would hurry. They disappeared from sight on the steps below. He blew out a long noisy breath and relaxed. He would give them ten minutes. That ought to be time enough.

He settled back with the cigar clenched cockily between his teeth and congratulated himself. He had thought of everything.

Almost.

It was the purse-mouthed clerk in the license bureau who questioned Noelia's age. "She's got to be eighteen to get a license on her own. This little girl has got to have her parents' permission."

Witt groaned.

Smokey, thinking his intrigue was well in hand, reached for his hat, bobbled the cigar between his lips, and walked out of the room into the hall. He threw back his shoulders and strode confidently into his office.

Roseanne nearly tackled him. "It's about time, Smokey! You're harder to get hold of than a greased pig!"

Smokey flashed her a bright smile. He figured he could afford it. "Howdy, Roseanne . . . Seyton, Possom." He slipped behind his desk. "I expect you all are ready to get down to business?"

Seyton rose to the occasion, launching into a rehearsed speech on the tragedy of senility.

Roseanne listened in fidgety silence for exactly thirty seconds. "Oh, shut up, Seyton! You're as long-winded as Floyd on a Sunday morning!"

Seyton drooped into a pouty silence. Roseanne made a motion of rolling up her sleeves. "Let's get this show on the road."

Smokey swiveled his chair toward the window and peered casually over his shoulder at the street. The Rolls-Royce was still at the curb. He swung back around and said, with what he hoped was convincing impatience, "Wonder what's holding Clara up. I told her to have that paperwork ready first thing this morning."

"She's had all the time in the world," Seyton muttered accusingly.

Smokey fired up his well-licked cigar and sent a tremendous cloud of fine blue haze boiling toward the ceiling. "Why don't you folks just sit tight and I'll find out what's keeping her?" He rolled his chair back and sauntered into Clara's office. With a flick of his elbow he nudged the door shut behind him.

"Witt ought to be out of there by now!" he hissed into Clara's upturned face. "Get down to the clerk's office and see what the hell's going on!"

Clara slipped into the hallway without a word, leaving Smokey behind gnawing the end of his cigar to shreds.

"Well?" he demanded when she returned a minute later.

"They're waiting on her parents. The girl's not eighteen!"

"Oh, Christ!"

There was a loud rap at the closed door.

"Start typing!" Smokey whispered frantically.

Another thunderous knock. "Smokey! You in there?" It was Seyton's voice.

"Put some paper in your machine for God's sake!" Smokey snapped under his breath. Clara's fingers fed an old courthouse bulletin into the typewriter and began pounding away at the keyboard. Seyton yanked open the door and peered in. His face was darkly suspicious.

Smokey wheeled around, managing to flash Seyton a reassuring smile while blocking his view of the typewriter. He cupped Seyton's elbow firmly in his hand and steered him back through the doorway. "Won't be a minute, and Clara'll have the order all typed up and ready to sign. Meantime, how's about some coffee?"

Without waiting for an answer he fished the thermos out of his desk and filled three Dixie cups. Another furtive glance through the window—still no sign of the girl's parents.

Clara's typewriter was ricocheting from behind her closed door like a machine gun spraying wild. He passed a cup across his desk, answering Roseanne's poisonous scowl with a forced smile. "That Clara can really set them keys on fire when she sets a mind to it," he mumbled inanely, barely catching himself in time from wondering aloud what in the world she could be typing.

Clara's rat-a-tat punctuated the dragging minutes . . . ping-bang . . . ping-bang . . . ping-bang . . .

Possom stood up, restless in the uneasy atmosphere.

Smokey was on his feet like a shot. "Here, have a stogie!" he shouted, unable to control his voice. He snapped out a cigar to lure him away from the window. It was too late.

206

Possom had spotted the Rolls-Royce. His eyebrows traveled halfway up his forehead. "Roseanne . . . ?" he began.

Smokey trampled him with his voice. "Goddammit, Clara, are you going to take till doomsday on that thing?"

The typing stopped.

The sudden silence shook Roseanne and Seyton. They stretched their necks toward Clara's door.

The judge's mouth went dry. In another second Possom was going to tell Roseanne about Witt's car. Smokey swallowed the wad of cotton in his throat and made his unhappy decision: "Clara!" he yelled. "If that thing's ready, get it in here *pronto!*"

Roseanne and Seyton were staring at the door as if they expected the lady or the tiger.

"Roseanne . . ." Possom said again.

She waved him off, batting her hand in the air, never giving him a glance.

The door flew open and Clara emerged with the papers. Roseanne's hand shot out for them.

"But, Roseanne . . ." Possom tried again.

Her eyes flashed fire. "For Christ's sake, Possom, can't you stay out of my hair for one short minute? Now, shut up and sit down!"

Possom shrank back as if he had been slapped. He turned toward the window and stared down at the street. One time too many, he thought . . . you've gone and told me to shut up one time too many.

He watched Witt's car, not knowing what its presence outside meant but sensing it was somehow significant—a situation that would keenly interest Roseanne. "Okay, Roseanne," he said to himself, soothing his hurt by talking back to her in his silent, interior fashion. "You have it your way. I ain't saying another word."

Smokey caught the change in Possom. For an instant their eyes met, and the judge knew that for some unfathomable reason Possom was going to hold his tongue. Then Possom looked back at the street.

Smokey followed his gaze. An old pickup had rolled up beside the Rolls-Royce. Its back end was loaded with festively dressed youngsters hanging over the tailgate. Already out of the cab and hurrying up the sidewalk were a man and a woman attired as for church . . . or a wedding!

Smokey turned, a wide smile spreading like warm butter across his face. Roseanne was hunched over the papers, her finger underlining the words. "Read it over carefully," he urged, wiping his forehead. "We want to be sure everything's in running order."

Roseanne gave an impatient wave. "I can't concentrate as long as you keep yapping."

Smokey's voice was oily. "Take your time, Roseanne, just take your own sweet time."

Witt's Rolls-Royce turned the corner, sailing out of sight, just as Roseanne, Seyton, and Possom stepped into the sunlight at the top of the courthouse steps. Roseanne clutched the order in her hands, trusting neither of the men with her future.

"Well," Seyton breathed. "We got that over with. Ol' Smokey fell right in line."

"That ain't nothing, honey," Roseanne said. Her face was tough. "The fun is just beginning. We're going to need the sheriff and a good strong straitjacket to wrassel Witt kicking and screaming to the head doctor."

Possom said nothing, but he looked like a man who knew a secret and wasn't going to tell.

"Let's get started," Roseanne said briskly. "First step is to

208

go out to his ranch and try to get his co-operation. Then when he raises a ruckus, we can call the sheriff."

San Pablo's sacristy was packed with Noelia's relatives. They perched on folding chairs, roosted on windowsills, and lined the walls. When Katie and Colbert arrived, there was an excited whisper around the room. A child was coaxed from his chair and Katie took her seat in the back.

Father Anselmo was beside himself. The prayed-for hour was near. Noelia would be married. No more visions. No more trouble. He hovered over his lectern and cast repeated impatient glances at his watch.

At last the wedding party drove up. The children swarmed into the sacristy. Carmen followed, grinning broadly across her flat face, puffing laboriously. Hector shuffled up and down the crowded rows of folding chairs and then made the circuit of the walls and windows, shaking every man's hand.

Suddenly the women let out a long, appreciative *Aaah!* Noelia had appeared in the doorway, glowing in her crisp white finery. Her eyes darted quickly about the room, taking everyone in, before she dropped the lacy veil over her face. She floated like a ruffled swan into the room.

Witt followed behind her. Katie bit her lip and rolled her eyes ceilingward at the sight of his tie. Colbert elbowed his way through the crowd and joined him.

Father Anselmo bustled back and forth, arranging the bride and groom in front of the lectern. Then, all smiles and bobbing up and down in a series of happy bows, he said, "Ah yes, we are all here. We are ready to begin." He looked down at his missal, noticing with momentary horror that it lay open to the graveside service. He smiled apologetically for the delay and thumbed through the pages until he came to the nuptial service. It would be short. There was to be no Mass.

With a polite cough to start things off, he carved the sign of the cross in the air above the couple and began the ceremony.

Roseanne was told the bad news by Witt's gate guard at the ranch.

"*Seyton!* Does this mean what I think it means?"

Seyton nearly gagged on his words. "Drive back to town quick! We got to stop that wedding! If Witt gets married to that girl, we just get shoved one rung too many down the next-of-kin ladder!"

Roseanne sagged and went pale. "You mean . . . ?"

Possom, sitting alone in the back seat, could keep silent no longer. He leaned forward until he could see Roseanne's face. "What he means, honey, is that if Witt marries his little friend, you can take that court order and use it to wipe your fanny!"

Father Anselmo droned on in Latin, sounding for all the world to Witt like a cattle barn auctioneer. Katie giggled when Witt ducked as the priest shook holy water above their heads. Witt silenced her with a dark, over-the-shoulder glower.

Father Anselmo called for the ring. Witt looked up in pain. "I . . . I . . ." he mumbled.

"Here!" It was Katie's voice from the back. She was pulling at her finger. She pushed forward between two children and slipped her ring into Witt's palm. "Be my guest," she whispered in his ear. "I aim to get me another."

Witt gave her a long cozy wink, and the priest gasped despite himself. He recovered and started to continue.

From outside a terrible squeal of braking tires brought everything to a halt.

210

Witt looked into the priest's eyes. "Quick!" he barked. "Get this over *pronto!*"

Father Anselmo crossed himself and plunged on.

Roseanne charged the sacristy and threw open the door just as the priest intoned: "Señor Tyler, you may kiss your bride."

Witt did. Then he looked over his shoulder and grinned at Roseanne, swaying gray as death in the doorway. For an instant he let her take in the scene. Then, as his old dream flashed through his mind, he cupped one hand around his mouth and let loose the wettest, loudest, most obscenely rattling raspberry of his entire life. Father Anselmo spent the rest of the day in bed.

CHAPTER TWENTY

They left the church and drove to Rockpoint to a rented cottage on a sloping, grassy bluff. It was nestled in an open grove of windswept live oaks, from which they had a clear view of the bay. It was the first time Noelia had ever seen the sea. Witt took her—he still in his dark blue suit, she in her wedding dress—along the narrow crescent of shell-strewn beach.

Rubber-booted surf fishermen, trying their luck at that afternoon hour, raised their eyes and stared in polite astonishment at the strangely dressed couple who strolled along the waterside.

"Howdy," Witt called into the sea wind as they passed. "Any luck?"

Like vendors displaying wares, the fishermen hauled in their short lines attached to their belt loops and hoisted their dripping catch into the air.

"Trout," Witt explained to Noelia. "Seems like everybody's catching trout."

Noelia, who was ignorant of the name for any fish, was stirred with pride at Witt's knowledge of the sea. She slipped her arm proprietorially into his as if by contact she could catch the overflow of his lore. When they next passed a man standing hip deep in the gently foaming surf she herself called out, "Any luck?" To her delight he raised three glistening fish above the swells, turning them slowly so the sun glinted off their silvery liquid sequins.

"Trout," she said, smug in her pride. Although they were drum, not trout after all, Witt squeezed her hand and said, "Yep."

The cottage was cozily furnished with a red brick fireplace along one wall, although it was too warm for a fire. They sat before the open window in yellow lamplight as the sun sank into the horizon behind them and ate boiled shrimp and homemade bread the proprietor's wife brought to their door.

Beneath the darkening sky, pale phosphor chains marbleized the backs of purple waves. There was a lull as the wind took a breath, adjusting to the temperature change. For a moment, from the window, they could hear the breakers sliding up the beach and sinking with a whisper beneath the packed, crushed shells. Then the wind came again, salty and cool, carrying with it the green, wet scent of seaweed and shellfish, rattling the thrown-back wooden shutters, and billowing the thin cotton curtains.

Noelia cleared the tiny table where they had eaten and disappeared into the bedroom to change, leaving Witt at the window to watch the winking yellow lights from the slender finger islands that rose out of the bay half a mile offshore. The pinpoints flickered, waned, then blazed again like hovering fireflies. Beyond, in the open waters of the Gulf, another string of lights, ghostly white, slid southward toward the horizon. He strained his ears into the wind, trying to catch the voice of the ship, but it slipped silently out of sight.

Noelia's shadow fell across him. He looked up smiling and caught her hand. Her hair, freed from its plaits, fell over the shoulders of her nightgown. He switched off the table lamp and drew her down beside him.

They stayed there a week. By the end Noelia could distinguish drum from trout, having caught both herself. She scrutinized the tides, making sure they performed on schedule, and collected sand dollars, seashells, and cast-up bottles, which she filled with wild flowers and arranged on the cottage's windowsills.

Toward the end of their stay, Witt chartered a small vessel to take them out into the deeper waters of the Gulf so Noelia could say she had been there. She had been happy and excited as they set out, but as soon as land dropped below the pitching horizon she turned ghastly pale and clung to his arm, panting heavily until he ordered the boat back to shore. Before they could make it into port she became violently sick. He cradled her white face in his hands and stroked her hair, trying to soothe her with gentle words; but the nausea persisted throughout the day, long after they had docked; and she went to bed early that night with a wet cloth wrapped around her throat.

The next morning she said she was well, though her cheeks were still wan and she had no appetite. She imagined she had shamed Witt by becoming sick and she apologized for not being a sailor. He comforted her by saying that it didn't matter, that there wasn't much water on his ranch anyway.

The next day they left for the ranch.

On both sides of the highway home the plains stretched away from them in an unbroken expanse. The sun balanced like a flattened ball on the western rim. It burned through the horizon's ragged clouds, setting them afire. All else was emptiness.

Suddenly, they came upon it! All at once, out of nowhere,

it leaped toward the pale sky as if the flat, monotonous countryside had cracked open and thrust a chunk of itself upward—a dark, blunt mesa crouching magnificently above the land.

Witt whooped with joy. "Just look at my mountain, Noelia!"

He braked the car and they climbed out. They stared breathlessly across the fields at the pyramid as if they had never seen it before, as if they had burst upon an undiscovered wonder in an unexplored land.

They watched without a word, too moved to speak, until the sun dropped beneath the horizon and the incandescent clouds cooled to gray ash. Reluctantly they got back in the car and headed on.

Once more, as they turned south on the highway that skirted the ranch, Witt pulled onto the shoulder and doused the headlights. Noelia sat sideways in the seat with her legs tucked under her and her head against his chest. He stroked the back of her neck, but his eye stared through the windshield at the pyramid.

"They're building fast," he murmured. "They ought to be finished by spring."

He continued to watch for a long time until he became aware by the soft regularity of Noelia's breath that she had fallen asleep. He moved gingerly, starting the car without disturbing her, but as he reached for the lights she opened her eyes and made a sound, a drowsy groan of protest. Her head snuggled closer against his chest.

"Are you okay, baby?"

"So sleepy. Let's stay here for a while."

But Witt put the car in gear and steered onto the road. He kept one hand on the wheel and held her close with the other. "We'll be home in a couple of minutes. You can wait that long, can't you?"

215

She nodded into his chest. But by the time they reached the ranch house she had dozed off again. He gathered her into his arms and lifted her from the car. She awoke and locked her hands behind his neck. Without either of them having thought about it, Witt found himself carrying his bride over the threshold.

Katie was leaving. She called Witt to tell him she had bought her ticket to Chicago. The next day he drove into town and met her at the depot. The train was late and she slipped into the front seat beside him to wait.

"I can't believe you're really leaving," he murmured after she offered her cheek to be kissed.

She rattled her bracelets impatiently and squinted out the window at the dusty little town. "I ought to have my head examined for sticking around so long! This rinkydink depot marks the start and stop of it all, you know. First place I laid eyes on when McIntosh brought me here, and then . . ."

Witt saw her face pale suddenly beneath the pink rouged circles. He knew she was remembering Wally and the casket. He wanted to say something, anything, to change the subject, but the arriving train's sharp whistle had already distracted her. They both glanced down the track, then quickly toward each other.

"This is it," she whispered. She grabbed his hand, appalling Witt by looking suddenly frail. She recovered almost immediately and thrust out her chin. Tossing her yellow hair out of her eyes, she let go of him and reached for the door.

They stood side by side on the quaking platform as the train rocked to a halt. Witt carried her baggage into the Pullman.

He was glad to see she had booked a drawing room. "At least you're traveling in style."

She dropped her purse on the seat and threw up the window shade. "Only the best for the Queen of the Mountain!"

He laughed and joined her at the window. Together they looked out at the street, deserted in the noontime heat. The train wheezed, spraying steam onto the platform. Katie began to sing, softly, in an almost tuneless chant: "Make my bed, light my light; I'll be home late tonight. Bye-bye, Landry. . . ." She paused, then went on quietly as a sigh, ". . . bye-bye, Landry; bye-bye, Wally; bye-bye, Witt."

Witt straightened up. "Don't forget McIntosh."

She nodded dutifully. "Yeah, bye-bye, McIntosh. I'm glad it's you and not me that's buried down here."

She turned to face him. "God! I could stand a stiff drink!"

The conductor called the all-aboard.

Witt searched her eyes. "What's up ahead?"

"Well, I'm still staring forty in the face." She gave him a long look, daring him to deny it. "I'm going to find me the richest bachelor in Chicago and show him what he's been missing all these years."

It made Witt happy. "Don't fall for the first Valentino that comes along promising to take you to Mexico."

"You bastard," she whispered. "I ought to spit in your eye for that, but it's the only one you've got."

He grinned.

"All aboard!"

They looked at each other intently.

"Noelia says *adiós* . . . and thanks for the ring."

"I'm glad she's wearing it."

"Don't stay away forever. Come back and visit us."

She stood on her toes and brushed his lips with hers. "Bye, honey. Stay on top of that mountain!"

"You, too!"

She nodded and wheeled away . . . too abruptly.

217

Witt stood there for a moment, then ducked quickly out of the room.

He waited on the platform until the train pulled away. Katie was at the window. He raised his hat in farewell. She blew him a kiss. He could see that she was crying; so was he.

Dr. Koury seemed to be taking forever with Noelia's examination. Witt paced the other office letting the cup of coffee the nurse had brought grow cold. He kept telling himself that whatever Koury might find wrong with Noelia, he was a good enough doctor to set things right again. After all, hadn't he patched him up until he felt good as new?

He stopped by the window and looked out. It was a bright autumn day, warm, with a high sun and no wind. Buildings blocked his view; nearby the post office and city hall, farther on St. Catherine's red tile roof and belfry. But he knew that beyond was his pyramid, rising higher each day. He scarcely cared.

He could think of nothing but Noelia. He started at every footstep in the corridor outside, looking up to meet Koury, preparing himself in case he brought bad news. But the footsteps always moved on, leaving him with long minutes to fret and pace. Now there was another sound beyond the door. Witt backed up against the windows.

Koury entered.

He was nodding to Witt as if he had already said something.

Witt cleared his throat. He couldn't tell anything from Koury's face. "Well," he said, hating to ask. "What's the story, Doc?"

Koury smiled. "You better order a box of cigars. She's going to have a baby."

Witt blinked. For an instant he was perfectly still. Then

218

he threw back his head and whooped, a rebel yell that brought Noelia flying into the room, her dress still opened at the back.

"Señor!" she cried. Her bright eyes half scolded him for the ruckus.

Still whooping at the top of his lungs, he lifted her by the waist and swept her in wild circles around the room.

"Hey, hey, take it easy," Koury called. "You've got to be gentle with her now."

Witt spun to a stop but kept her in his arms. He was laughing dizzily. He couldn't stop.

Koury sat on the edge of the desk and grinned.

Witt sailed his hat across the room. "I'm the happiest man in the world, Doc!" He looked down at Noelia and ran his fingers over her cheek. "I knew we could do it, honey. I knew it all along!"

"Congratulations," Koury said.

Witt grabbed his hand. "I've got no words to thank you with, Doc."

Koury shook his head. "No need to."

"Sure there is!" He shook his head in appreciation of the wonderful pink pills. "Doc, believe me, I'm . . . I'm beholden. I don't guess I'll ever be able to repay you."

Instead of going home, Witt and Noelia walked to the bank. Albert Pugh, following the late Billy Hale's example, sprang forward with a glad hand to greet them.

"Let me see my safety-deposit box," Witt said. "It's been a long time since I looked in on it."

"Sure thing, Witt," Albert purred.

They pushed through the gate to the vault. "I guess you want to use the back office, huh?"

"Not this time," Witt said. "I'll open it right here."

219

Albert's eyebrows shot up.

Witt had already produced his key. Albert cast a discretely curious eye downward as they turned the lock. Witt flipped back the lid.

The box held three objects, the deed to Witt's ranch, his oil royalties contract, and a small blue velvet case. Witt withdrew the case and pressed the latch.

Albert gasped.

Inside, blazing like a brushfire, was the biggest diamond stickpin he had ever seen.

"Jesus Christ!" he murmured in awe. "So it's true!"

The stone could have covered his thumbnail. Its icy facets caught the overhead light and shot it back into his eyes like a splintered rainbow.

"Señor!" Noelia cried. "Is it real?"

"Damn right, it's real. No hunk of glass sparkles like that." He took the pin from the case and held it up, rolling it between his fingers. Albert marveled that anything burning so fiercely wasn't too hot to touch.

Witt drove the pin through his tie and fastened it. "Pretty thing, isn't it?"

"Goddamn!" Albert breathed. "You ain't going to wear it, are you?"

"You bet your boots, I am," Witt said. He looked down at his chest and tugged at the tie until he was satisfied. Then he turned to face the lobby.

The bank had fallen silent, all eyes on him since he opened the box. The diamond flashed from his chest, as piercing and blue-white as his unblinking eye.

Betty Jean Schneider's mouth sagged and she lost track of the bills she was counting out. Behind her a tray of coins crashed to the floor, ringing like nervous bells. Her customer, too astonished to do anything else, broke into giggles.

Satisfied with the effect, Witt nodded to Noelia and said, "Now, baby, let's take a little walk."

As amazed as everyone else in the lobby, she obeyed dumbly. She slipped her arm through his and let herself be led from the bank.

The Main Street business section was eight blocks long. They set out, strolling leisurely toward the far end. Their parade began quietly, but word raced ahead of them. Gawkers crammed into doorways hoping to catch a glimpse of the fabled diamond; it glared back at them like a blinding headlamp, catching fire in the bright sunlight.

"Señor, everybody's looking," Noelia whispered.

"Fine and dandy. That's what I want them to do. Morning, Charlie; morning, Earl." He tipped his hat to two men hanging out in a doorway.

He and Noelia walked on, letting everyone see. Out of Budd's Jewelry Store came Sam Budd himself, jeweler's loupe in hand, hoping for a better look. Witt kept his stride. He nodded and spoke, but left Budd behind, frustrated and disappointed.

They covered the eight full blocks until nothing remained ahead but filling stations and used car lots. He started to cross the street to walk back up the other side. Noelia, her arm looped through his, felt him hesitate.

"One more block, baby," he said, looking straight in front. "There's one other person I want to show this to."

Noelia started to ask who, but she followed his gaze. In the middle of the next block, pulling into Hooper's Used Car Lot was Roseanne's big green Cadillac.

Possom spotted them first. Roseanne was already half out of the car when he mumbled excitedly to her and pointed down the sidewalk where Witt and Noelia were advancing. Roseanne seemed to go to pieces, as if half of her wanted to crawl back into the car while the other half still insisted on getting out. The struggle dropped her with an awkward thud on the blacktop beside the car.

Witt could hear her muttered curses as she picked herself up and scrambled back into the seat, slamming the door behind.

Possom had jumped out and run around the car when Roseanne fell.

"Howdy, Possom," Witt called. "Reckon Roseanne hurt herself?"

Possom reached for the door, ignoring him.

Witt stooped and gave Roseanne a playful wave through the closed glass. Her head jerked away from the window.

"What's the matter, Possom? Roseanne doesn't look too hot."

"What more do you want, Witt? You want to rub our noses in it?"

Witt straightened up. "I don't follow you, Possom."

There was a noise to their left, a wooden door opening and slamming with a bang. They both looked across as Wild Bill Hooper bounded from his office shed and scurried across the black pavement in a determined beeline for Possom.

"Hi, there, Possom!" he shouted, extending his hand while he was still a good ten yards off. "I got your message. Is this the Caddy-lack you're trying to sell me?"

He grabbed Possom's hand and wrenched it up and down, all the while appraising Roseanne's car out of the corner of his eye.

Suddenly Witt understood. He backed away. "Give them a good price, Wild Bill," he said. He didn't know the details but by the grim set of Possom's face he figured they needed it.

Wild Bill glanced over. "Why, hidee, Witt . . . good God, man! What in the world is that thing on your tie?"

Witt didn't reply. He saw Roseanne looking at him now, staring at the diamond in bitter defeat.

He turned away quickly. The game was over. Somehow Roseanne had slipped and he had dragged her across the line. It was her game, she had started it, but why in the hell did she have to lose so pitifully? He dragged Noelia away, crossing the street, leaving them behind to sell their car.

Noelia was moving at a run to keep up with him.

"Goddamn Roseanne!" he muttered. "She's not even decent enough to let a person enjoy winning. Ashes . . . ashes in my mouth!"

When they reached the car outside Koury's office, Witt put Noelia in the front seat and told her to wait for him. He disappeared inside. He was away only a minute. When he stepped back through the door his collar was open and both the tie and the diamond had vanished. He stood for a moment on the sidewalk before sliding in behind the wheel.

Noelia sat up on her knees in the seat. "Señor! Your diamond, what happened to it?"

He looked down at his chest as if he too were surprised to see it gone. Then he shrugged. "I gave it away. I gave it to Doc. I thought it was the least I could do to thank him properly."

Noelia nodded. It was simple truth.

He started the engine and headed out of town. When they reached the open highway, he smiled suddenly, remembering something. "You should've seen Doc's face when I gave it to him. I took the whole thing off, tie and all, and handed it over . . . but all wadded up so he couldn't see the diamond. Well, he thought I was just giving him the tie and he thanked me nicely for it."

He laughed out loud at this little joke. "But then he felt the diamond. Oh, Lordie, I should have taken you with me so you could have seen his face when he finally laid eyes on it. Course he swore up and down he wouldn't accept it. I had to sweet-talk him into it. I had to promise that if I ever take a notion I want it back, all I have to do is ask."

He was silent for a moment, watching the pyramid growing in size as they approached the ranch. Then he added, "Someday Doc is going to try to give that diamond back to you . . . you know, someday when I'm not around to say no. But I don't want you to take it, do you hear?"

Noelia nodded.

"No matter what he says, I don't want you to take it back. I gave it to him and it's his. I figure he's given us something better."

CHAPTER TWENTY-ONE

That night at the ranch Witt threw a fiesta. Like a happy king decreeing public jollity, he summoned Colbert and told him to stop all work on the pyramid for twenty-four hours. Then he called into town and ordered a truckload of beer, which Hector packed in long ice-filled trenches. The bunk-house cooks sweetened the air with the aroma of spitted beef sizzling over open coals. At sunset, for the first time since work had begun, the ring of floodlights remained dark around the pyramid, allowing night shadows to cover the land.

On the porch, in the unfamiliar darkness, Noelia snuggled closely beside Witt, blessed by heaven, looking on as every-one reveled in their good fortune.

Witt felt a giddy wave flood through his body, a bubbling joy that filled his being, finding room to grow and expand as if his soul had infinite capacity.

He didn't need to tell this to Noelia. She felt it in the pressure of his hand, saw it in the smile that played across his lips, an odd smile, untroubled, peaceful, contented, and fulfilled. It was only just visible in the stray light from an open window behind them, but even in that light its meaning was unmistakable.

The moon rose very late, a fine-drawn, graceful crescent

like a half coil of silver filigree among the stars. The workmen, their stomachs filled, their brains drowsed by beer, had drifted off to their bunks or lay beneath the wheeling spangled sky beside the warmth of the dying coals, and slept.

A tranquil stillness settled over the ranch. No lights, no rumbling engines, no movement. Only the regular sighing of the oil pumps, heard again—after so long—soft and airy. They played counterpoint to Noelia's warm breath as she lay in Witt's arms.

Then he began to sing, a voice surprisingly strong. It lifted above the darkness and soared out across the open fields. It was the only song he knew; out of all the songs and ballads he had sung in his youth, it was the only one that came back to him. He sang to Noelia.

> Come and sit by my side if you love me;
> Do not hasten to bid me adieu.
> Just remember the Red River Valley
> And the cowboy who loved you so true.

When he finished, he kissed her on the forehead, a loving touch that reached the baby growing inside her.

She passed her fingers over his cheeks, over the creases and the gray stubble, over the broken nose and the empty eye, and said, "I love you, Señor."

The moon sailed higher.

He could tell by the pressure her body exerted against him that she was drifting between sleep and wakefulness. He put his fingers in her hair and said, "Run on to bed, baby."

"I'll stay with you, Señor."

He shook his head. "No, you run on. You're sleepy. I'll be there in a minute. I just want to sit out here and watch till the moon reaches the top of its run."

226

She rubbed her cheek against his chest and rose. The door closed softly behind her.

He crossed his arms and sat back in his chair extending his long legs and curling his toes in his boots. He was comfortable, he thought . . . he could sleep right there.

The moon approached the zenith. Its blue-white rays settled like fine silver drizzle on the pyramid's steel beams, outlining the shape with ghostly light.

Witt stared.

Suddenly the black spaces between the beams were no longer dark sky. They became stone bound together by the moonlight's mortar, reminding him of the slaty afterimage he had first seen.

He opened his eye with a start. Had he been dreaming? The moon still hung at the top of the sky. And the pyramid was there . . . solid and complete, a finished monument . . .

He drifted off again.

The field stretching out before him was cool and green. A mellow breeze ruffled the tall grass billowing it like sea waves. Noelia stood in the distance knee-deep in the rolling meadow. Open dewy roses twined through her hair.

"Look, Señor," she called to him. She reached down and raised a small child by his arms. For a moment she held him out toward Witt. Then she lifted the baby high onto her shoulder. "Wave!" she urged. She gave his tiny arm a nudge of encouragement. "Wave to Papa."

The baby's wide, clear eyes swept the field.

"Wave!"

At last the child saw Witt and he waved.

Tears of joy trickled down Witt's seamed cheeks. They ran wetly into the deep creases and caught in the stubble of his whiskers.

The baby laughed, a bright innocent sound of pleasure and satisfaction at his trick.

Witt wanted to raise his arm to wave back to his son; indeed he thought he had. His smile broadened.

"Call him Witt," he thought he said. "Call my boy Witt."

And he could see Noelia in the cool, green field nodding . . .

And so the pyramid was finished, as Witt had dreamed. On the first day of spring, before a cheering crowd who streamed through the gate onto the ranch, the four-sided capstone was hoisted into place. The steeply slanted sides soared toward the hot blue sky, each granite wall dazzling bright in the sun at high noon.

The mayor spoke from a platform at the base. Colbert cut a ribbon that stretched across the dizzying stair path marching upward to the tip. Then, at Noelia's request, the high school band massed beside the pyramid and played "Red River Valley."

As the music drifted over the land Noelia moved to the edge of the porch, where she had been watching. She held her breath. She could almost hear Witt singing along. She closed her eyes and pretended he was standing beside her.

That night, after the crowds had dwindled away, Colbert came for her. His crew of six men had already unearthed Witt's coffin from its burial place beside the house and loaded it onto the old pickup. Colbert nodded to the foreman and the truck started toward the pyramid. He and Noelia followed on foot. As they came to the gate at the lawn's edge, Noelia paused and plucked a handful of spring roses from the bushes blooming along the fence.

When they reached the pyramid, the men slid the coffin from the pickup and carried it to a narrow niche in the wall.

Then, gingerly and solemnly, into the crypt, they laid Witt to rest.

A slab of matching granite was eased into the opening. Noelia took the trowel and smoothed the mortar around the edges. On the slab, Colbert had carved:

WITT TYLER BUILT THIS.

Noelia then laid the rude bouquet at the base below the crypt and started back for the house. When she reached the fence at the edge of the lawn, she turned for a last farewell to Witt. As she lifted her hand, she paused and placed it over her belly. Their baby was stirring.

FIC Jos   Joseph, Ro   c.2
The monument maker.
ATH AF   [1st ed.]   1972.

Athens Regional Library System

3 3207 00125 8542